THE COMFORT

Hylke Speerstra

The Comfort Bird

www.hylkespeerstra.nl

Original title: De Treastfûgel
Translated from Frisian by Prof. Henry J. Baron

Cover photography:
frech, Philip McErlean, USFWS Steven Tucker

This translation was made possible in part with support from the
Province of Fryslân.

Mokeham Publishing Inc. - 2017
P.O. Box 35026, Oakville, ON L6L 0C8, Canada
P.O. Box 559, Niagara Falls, NY 14304, USA
www.mokeham.com

ISBN: 978-0-9919981-1-1

EXPLANATORY NOTE on Frisian and Dutch and the spelling of the names of people and places.

This book was translated from its original Frisian text. Frisian is a minority language spoken in the northern Netherlands by about half a million people. It is a Germanic language, closely related to Dutch, German and English. It is considered by linguists to be the closest relative of English still spoken today. Frisian has a rich oral tradition and literary history.

In recent decades the language has received recognition in the Netherlands as the second national language and may be used in the province of Fryslân ('Friesland' in Dutch), in courts of law and government. This recognition was hard fought and for most of the period in which this book is set, Frisian would have been the language commonly spoken by the protagonists among each other. Conversations with people in authority would have taken place in Dutch. Dutch would also have been the language of school, church and government.

In this book we have chosen to use the Frisian form of personal and geographic names over the Dutch form. For ease of reference we have made an exception for larger or well-known towns and cities and for the name of the province itself. We have used the local form for names of towns outside of Friesland, even if a Frisian form exists.

PROLOGUE

PROLOGUE

A DARK DAY IN JANUARY. The stormy northwester drags one shower after another across the bare flatlands. What no one thinks can possibly happen anymore does: Friesland can no longer handle all her water. Thus the old land once more becomes immersed. The first small inner dikes succumb; glistening strips already begin to appear here and there in the pale green. It brings me back to the time when the voice of the water was still feared and understood.

It was in the Second World War; I was the farm child that would always remain a part of me. I'm back in the hamlet of Iemswâlde where I was born and grew up. On a head-neck-rump farm along a mile-long, dead-end gravel road. A neighborhood of seven farms, a dairy, a couple of worker's homes, and a bridge house.

A long winter without color, flooded fields, in late winter an unannounced cold spell, steel-blue skies, frozen over canals form endless ice roads, skating under a full moon. The people in hiding with us (our 'divers') tell us that German soldiers have weak ankles and are no good on skates, so we tie our skates on and take an advance on freedom. We skate around the farm in ever wider circles. In moonlight you can skate even faster than your own shadow. Silver swarms of bombers in V-formation sing high above us, and we hum along: "And by the clear moonlight, we bomb Berlin at night."

It's almost seventy years later; this stormy January 3, 2012, can no longer wrest itself free from the dusk and the memory. The northwester is blowing harder, and it blows me back to the haymow where the divers have their hideouts; I know only the alias of most. The Jew is Douwe Elzinga, the student from Leiden is Siebe, the dairy industry man from Bolsward is Ymte Heeg. By the bridge house on the Workum Canal, which otherwise is our entrance to the big outside world, a couple of divers stand on watch every night.

When evening falls and it's almost dark, the men dare to huddle together in the hay storage section of the barn that should still be half filled when the season moves toward the shortest day. I hear their voices, can still just make out their faces.

One day in Tsjerkwert when there's not enough fuel left to have all three of the stoves in the schoolhouse going, teacher Sjoerd Hibma comes to our hamlet to teach us, a man so tall and thin that according to Mother you could pull him through the glass of a kerosene lamp. In neighbor Jan Okkes Postma's cow barn covers hang behind the cows to catch the splashes of manure. We compute in our heads: "A cow carries for nine months. In which month does the farmer expect a calf if the cow was impregnated in mid-June?"

Underneath the rafters in the hayloft I join in listening to a performance that spills over with stories; out of a forbidden radio big, important words resound: Allied, Atlantic Ocean, Leningrad, Hitler, razzia.

An older diver, who one day suddenly makes his appearance and then another day suddenly disappears, climbs on top of a stack of straw bales which is turned into a kind of pulpit. Am I at neighbor Postma, Twynstra, or Buwalda? Not sure, but the man is a storyteller; we call him Uncle. His stories always start with the reading of a fragment from an old letter of an emigrant which he digs out of an old suitcase. The letter fragments are a bit like a Bible reading.

"Attention! I'm reading from a letter by William A. Elgersma from Sandstone, Minnesota, May 23, 1903. This letter was delivered in the Heidenskip in June of that year by the mailman from Workum. First it was read to old Elgersma, and still that same evening to William's old father-in-law Bauke Haitsma:

Dear Father, Brothers and Sisters,
Tjitske is doing a lot worse now and now I'm sitting alone
with her waiting for the doctor and because sometimes she
feels so uncomfortable, I just wanted to let all of you know.

I'm afraid worse times are still ahead since it looks now that
it's not going to last long anymore and I'm going to miss
my beloved wife and stay behind alone with my dear little
children. We are sorry to see in your letter that Lieuwkje
is changing her mind about coming here. We can't get a
housekeeper here and then what's going to happen to us?"

I listen and witness a live funeral, a farewell without a look back even once. I hear a scream for help in the dark midship of the steamship Noordam, see the homesickness curl from the chimney and blow away over the ocean. The still half-full hayloft changes into the shadowy middle deck of a ship on tall waves.

"And still after liberation I will step on the boat to America," says one, who has been in hiding, full of conviction. All around me brews a longing for long distances.

"My uncle the storyteller is just as well-traveled as Paul the Apostle," the dairy produce boss from Bolsward whispers to me. I believe him right away, because with his white beard and sad expression he is the spitting image of old Paul. That's how Rembrandt painted Paul in the history book of Bauke Buwalda's Sjoerd.

Uncle storyteller had left his town as a young man. He had torn himself loose, roots and all, from the tough Hichtum clay. The pain of that separation never went away. Worse, on the other side of the ocean it got worse. That was because Uncle had left his soul in Hichtum. After a life with a lot of adversity, worry, and homesickness he returned to his place of birth, only to discover that Hichtum was no longer the town that he had left. "The soil that once held my cradle was still as heavy and tough, but my roots could no longer flourish there."

Beneath the barn beams above the haymow, home-grown tobacco leaves are drying on tightly strung horse reins. The Virginia strain smells best. It's a waiting period till the time is ripe and the leaf becomes flaky, and then we're good to go. The divers roll cigarettes from the tobacco crumbs between thumb and forefinger, using the thin pages from the church hymnbook as rolling-paper. And that's how a hundred and fifty psalms and more than three hundred hymns go up in smoke. Not only that, the men taking delight in their mischief sing lustily, Psalm 79: "O how long against your people will your anger burn? O Lord, let your mercy on its flame be poured."

Our regular hired man Wiebe lifts me up so I can see the south-west through the roof window. I see silver strips of grasslands beneath low skies. Two villages – one with a pointed and the other with a stubby tower.

One morning the divers are gone. Uncle had left a few days earlier. There had been a razzia*. All the men had been able to escape in time through the field of the Buwaldas in the direction of the Sneek Canal, but that failed in Douwe's case, whose name was really Justin Gerstner. It was morning, after milking time; he had just changed into his dress clothes, and he could've just gotten away like that, but he changed his mind. He came back: "My milker's clothes, then I won't look like a Jew!" A bit later he hurried back again into the open fields, but it was too late now – he was caught. Douwe refused to tell the Germans with which Iemswâlde farmer he had been hiding, even after they had smashed nearly all his ribs with the butt of a gun. He persisted, didn't want to betray the family of Bauke Buwalda which had so warmly included him. Because Douwe knew it: the Buwaldas would be lined up against the wall and their farm would burn. They tore the pants off Douwe and mocked him mercilessly. Then they pushed him into a ditch in the fields. A gunshot sounded. A bullet through the neck, it turned out.

Farmer Bauke Buwalda, standing in his backyard, must have seen

---

* An organized round-up in which German occupation forces would cordon off a geographic area and systematically search door to door for people in hiding.

what happened. All the blood drained from his face. Powerless. "With his cap in his hand," declared his son Sjoerd and his cousin, diver Hessel Baarda, later. "It is the day that in the same Germany the words were nailed to a church door that penance would be exacted," Sjoerd said later that morning.

The tragic drama of Douwe, a gifted student, took place on Tuesday morning, October 31, 1944, at a quarter past eight. In just three months, the young man had learned to speak Frisian without an accent as well as to write it. Even more impressive: on St. Nicholas Eve, 1943, he had shared his firm conviction with all the others in sound Frisian: "One who walks around in a blue farmer's shirt and can milk with the best of them will not be seen as a Jew. I'm undertaking this escape because I want to live, I want to experience, I want to imagine, I want to feel, I want to survive."

Had they been betrayed? Who? Certainly not Uncle? Uncle was a wandering storyteller, without a home. Later on in the fall I heard that the divers had hidden farther on, in the town with the stubby tower. Someone dropped the village name, Hichtum. Hadn't Uncle come from there? Where did he end up?

After the raid and the sudden disappearance of the men in hiding, the door between our farmhouse and the world was no longer ajar, but closed. No longer any strangers in the yard. Hunger evacuees, who had risked a long journey over the Enclosure Dam separating the North Sea and IJssel Lake, do not advance beyond the iron gate. The small cow barn windows are darkened at the command of the occupier so that not a glimmer of light can shine through at night. The radio has been buried deep under the hay, awaiting the hour that Hitler will surrender.

Now and then a neighbor, bent over from the low ceilings of the Frisian cow barn, comes by for a chat. Hardly a word about news from the war front; even the death of Douwe goes unmentioned, as if the adults are ashamed that they weren't able to keep that fine fellow out of German hands. The only thing I hear is talk about the studbook, about the breed purity of the livestock. It's about breeding lines and a preference for bulls with peerage.

Are those cannons that boom in the distance? Or could it be severe weather, perhaps?

Under a new moon, by darkness, around 7:30 in the evening, neighbors come over for a cup of coffee every once in a while. Shiny medals hang on the wall, won in livestock competitions. The conversation is about the same legendary bulls, become immortal by their perfect structure and harmonious proportions, high feet and leg score, their scrotal circumference and testicular tone, pleasing temperaments, and an impressive pedigree. Is that how a silent hunger for art and beauty is compensated?

The seed of the cattle has been spread to all continents, but the farmer himself does not leave his yard because he has to go far to have a better life.

On April 17, 1945, the Canadians liberate my world. Today they are in Bolsward, so tomorrow they will be in Hichtum and Tsjerkwert. It is a mild and bright spring day, a day one can hear the grass grow and see the cows romp in the pasture. Blinded by the bright light and the new freedom, the cattle raise such a ruckus that some have blood running down their heads. Dad observes it from a distance, apparently unmoved; as long as he lives, he will not celebrate liberation. But he does wear a tie today and his new cap; today is his birthday, he is 42.

THE COMFORT BIRD

THE COMFORT BIRD

"Your mom has put her head down for the last time." Ytsje Wytsma is six when she hears these words from a neighbor. The children in the village explain to her what that means.

"Your mom is dead." A couple of days later the old stubby tower's bell tolls, announcing a woman's death. "If the tunes sound cheerful to you, your mother will go to heaven," the children said. "If they sound sad, she goes to hell."

That evening her dad puts her to bed for the first time. He promised to tell her a fairy tale, but it turns into a story without beginning or end. "My dear girl," Sibbele Wytsma stammers while he tucks her in, "fairy tales aren't real. Our work is going to have to pull us through."

And for farm laborer Wytsma there's enough work, enough to keep him busy for at least thirteen hours a day. It is hard toil on tough soil; the young widower comes home mostly just to sleep. When Ytsje is ten, Wytsma takes her out of school in Burchwert. Now she can be her dad's little housekeeper.

All of this is part of the grief of Hichtum in the extremely wet, late winter of 1861. The Leeuwarden paper reports that the high waters took thirty-seven lives. It is the year that serfdom was abolished in Russia and President Lincoln took the first step toward abolishing slavery in America. A steam train runs for the first time between Leeuwarden and Harlingen. Apparently in one of the cars a nasty passenger has hidden itself: cholera, targeting especially the poor. Possibly, Ytsje's mom was one of its victims.

"After the death of my mother, who in the end was suffering from seveer cramps, I fortunitely found a very good father," Ytsje would describe it much later.

She is brief when she entrusts her experiences to paper. And absolutely without self-pity. *"In a good three years of schooling I learned quite a bit so that I could still record something for my descendants, beyond that life is realy a play of happyness and grace."*

When she tries later to recall her mother, an image surfaces of a shadowy bedstead, a multi-colored pillow with a white face sunken into it. The enduring image of her dad is a *"bent-over man who, while constintly chewing, sits staring into nothing and now and again comments that his little girl is a wonderworker of a housekeeper."*

She doesn't get many carefree and sunny days coming her way, but the few she does, she will long remember. Take that mild and bright September day in that same year of 1861. The little housekeeper is ten and in between her work she goes searching through the fields for tufts of sheep's wool that are caught on field gates and barbed wires. It amounts to little more than fouled little pieces of wool, but the freedom of an open field and the collecting and gathering yield such sweet satisfaction. At home she washes the wool, spins it into thread, and is even able to knit it into underwear for herself and Dad. "She's a first-class wool gatherer," boasts Dad. Since the day his wife died Sibbele Wytsma addresses his daughter in the third person – from a you she's become a she.

"What are you standing there dreaming!" It is the child's voice of Meindert Boorsma, her friend from Hichtum who was her class-mate. "Come on, Ytsje, two can do more than one."

Meindert is an orphan who has adopted the old people language of his grandpa and grandma who are raising him. "Or are you not inclined to look for sheep's wool together with a neighbor boy?"

"Yes, of course."

"Actually, a charming girl like you should be going to school!" the boy said like a little adult.

"And what about you!"

"A boy like me can learn a lot from nature, from the birds of the field, says Grandpa." The little man comes from a family of bird catchers.

And that's how the boy and girl spend the whole beautiful September day searching for sheep's wool. "Ytsje, pay close attention to nature. Notice how the lapwings at the end of September begin to flock together. Does the girl know why the birds do that? They gather to make plans as migrating birds. They pose the question to themselves: Where shall we spend the winter, where and when should we commence the big journey? Today or tomorrow they will depart from us, and we from them."

"And next spring they will come back," adds his little female friend.

"Exactly. You're right. Listen, Ytsje. In the beginning of March we will see the first lapwings return, then they will entrust to us their nests and the first laying of their eggs. They do that because we as people of the field protect and take care of the meadow birds. We really are the housekeepers of the whole business. Do you know, Ytsje, that the first lapwing egg is always laid here before noon on March 19? That has to do with the light; the days are lengthening then. In March winter will still try to stay on its throne, but then the springtime can no longer be held back."

"How does he know all this?"

"I learned all these kinds of things from Grandpa. Right after the terrible hard winter of 1837 he found the first lapwing egg in the whole country, and do you know where it lay? Between two small ice floes in a ditch. It was in the field of Mensonides, and that's a man who records everything that happens through the weeks."

"Oh, my goodness." It's been as music to her ears.

"Well, my girl, that's enough for now. Yes. I like it too, you don't learn these things in school. This is how Grandpa thinks of it: the behavior of people has much in common with the migratory bird; both dislike short days and long shadows. But all right, a person is not a bird; a person cannot take his soul along like the migratory bird on long journeys across the ocean. That is why Grandpa avoids long ocean journeys."

Young Meindert Boorsma is not only named after this grandpa, he also bears his nickname: Meindert 'Birdie'.

On the day that the old Meindert became Grandpa, he made a

very special bird whistle for his namesake. He made it out of an ancient cow rib from the Hichtum terp*, a couple of tin copper plates, and a nail-hard knot of ebony wood. From that wood he carved the mouthpiece. When he tried it out he knew that it was good. The old man was already known then as the Stradivarius among bird whistle carvers. The little instrument was placed in the little boy's cradle in the hope that he would become just as sharp a field man as his forebears. At first the whistle brought only trouble; the mother died a few days later in the bed where she had given birth, while the father had already passed away the winter before.

When the old man first heard how lifelike his grandson could imitate the lapwing and later also the godwit and the redshank, he didn't believe at first that he wasn't listening to a real, living meadow bird.

For Ytsje and young Meindert the day of wool gathering comes to an end. It turns toward evening when the two saunter toward home with a bagful of sheep's wool. And then Meindert hears the call of the golden plover in the distance. "Come, they must not see us, let's crawl behind the field gate over there." The boy digs up his bird whistle and gives a kind of shy answer to the plover.

"Ytsje, I pretend to be a kind of insecure plover. I say that I don't dare to travel alone, that I'm a lost soul in need of help. I want them to take me along on their flight." Again Meindert puts his whistle to his lips, and then quite another song emerges.

"What are you doing now," Ytsje whispers sharply. "You're not imitating the golden plover but the lapwing. Why did you all of a sudden become a lapwing?"

"It's like this: with the bird migration another kind of bird accompanies nearly every flight of golden plovers." He's hardly got the words out of his mouth when a whole flock of birds streaks over

---

* A terp is an artificial mound, on which dwellings were built to keep them safe in times of floods. Many Frisian villages are built on terps.

them. "Look, this time there's a lapwing among them. Such a solitary one goes along as a comfort-giving bird. It's like Grandpa said: 'On dangerous travels one cannot do without a comforter.'"

Ytsje is still shy of twelve years old when she too suffers the lot that in these times afflicts almost all farm laborer daughters: to be placed with a farm family as a junior maid. One morning, around May 12, Dad takes her to the hamlet of Syswert below Hichtum. "I'm going to try to place you, if possible, with a gentleman famer there."

Father and daughter don't risk going to the front door, but call at the side door of the barn. Apparently the farmer has seen father and daughter coming, for he's right there. With his cap in hand, Sibbele Wytsma asks if the farmer and his wife can use his girl as a junior maid. And should that be the case, if they would be so kind as to take good care of her. "The child lost her mom when she was really too young to do without a mother."

The farmer says nothing. But there's the farmer's wife too. Wytsma addresses her now: "I can tell you this: this is a very responsible girl. I'm just asking if you can take it a little easy on her because she doesn't have a mother to run to anymore. As a farmworker who's busy all day I can't look after her." When Sibbele Wytsma has said his piece, an uncomfortable silence follows. A bit of light enters the barn through its small round windows.

"She's done an amazing job keeping house for me," Wytsma breaks the silence, "she's already learned how to milk by milking the goat."

"It's still a child, but for her age she has a pair of fleshy milking hands." That's the farmer.

"And even though I've had her in school for only a couple of years," Wytsma continues, "she's really good at reading and writing."

"We have no need of our workers reading the newspaper to us."

Sibbele Wytsma has learned to control himself.

"What are we going to do with such a child?" sighs the farmer's wife.

"We have our own rules here in Syswert," the husband continues. "We start milking at 4:15 in the morning."

Without saying another word, the father takes his child's hand and leaves the barn with her.

"I felt my hand swallowed inside Dad's warm," that's how Ytsje put it years later. "It felt to me as if Dad and I together walked toward spring. We were at least three fields farther, when I said: 'Dad, do you hear how beautifully the birds are singing?'

'No,' he said, 'I hear nothing that sounds like singing.'

'Don't you hear it?' I repeated. 'High above us the lapwing is singing.' And then I saw Dad cry for the first time. It was, if I remember it right, the 12th or 13th of May, 1862."

That same spring Ytsje is placed with a crop farmer below Arum. Here she doesn't have to milk. When Sibbele Wytsma finds out that his little daughter has to sleep in a wooden feeding trough in the back of the farm, he fetches her without wasting a word on it. "She better become Dad's housekeeper again."

At the end of October the mailman delivers a letter from the farmer in Syswert. *'The young girl can still come, to whit before milking time on All Saints Day.'*

There's a great likelihood that the preacher of the Reformed Church of Burchwert-Hichtum has gotten wind of the Syswert farmer's behavior. The quite socially minded Rev. Gysbert Duval Slothouwer had been there for decades as preacher, confidant, and pastor. As such Slothouwer was not averse to pulling for the underdog now and then. Later Ytsje will describe her Syswert farmer this way:

> *On All Saints Day I came to that farmer who, when push*
> *came to shove, was not all that saintly, though the wife*
> *was really not so bad. Besides, Rev. Duval Slothouwer told*
> *me that I could always come to him when something went*
> *wrong.*

22

A dark November 1 inside the milk barn. Milking time on All Saints. If the farmer is frugal, only three oil lamps will be hanging behind the long row of cows, but with farmers who are really tight, there'll be only one. And that is the case at Syswert. Left and right the new junior farm maid already hears the first squirts of milk.

"Look, behind those two small doors in the milk barn wall, that's your place at night," someone tells her. "Your bedstead." At first she doesn't notice that it's the voice of her wool-seeker friend.

"Birdie! Your voice has changed, it's almost like a man's voice now."

"That's a fact, my girl."

"And you've grown so tall."

"Yes, that's why you're getting my bed. I don't fit anymore. I said to the boss: 'I'm too big for the bedstead that's meant for little guys and also too big for the empty milk barn attic.' The boss said, 'When your wooden shoes are worn out, you'll fit easily underneath the milk barn attic.' I said, 'Grandpa told me that the Boorsmas don't have to bow before anybody.' The boss said, 'Damn you, All Saints will be your last day here.' And I said, 'That's not even such bad timing, boss, because I can start right away with a farmer in Hartwert who has the best cows in the whole area.'"

That same day, November 1, Meindert and Ytsje say goodbye to each other again. Her former wool-seeker friend does give her a good piece of advice: "Keep your bedstead doors closed at night, because if the cow right where you sleep shits or coughs when the doors are open, you're going to have manure visiting you."

The farmer and his wife were really fooled by that girl of twelve. Cows resistant to yielding their milk change under the hands of Ytsje Wytsma into easy-to-milk animals that let their milk flow freely, as if cast under a spell.

On New Year's Eve, 1863, Ytsje is promised a wage of a hundred guilders a year, including room and board. On top of that she receives a Christian education. On Sunday she's expected to go to the service in Hichtum. And in wintertime she may also attend the weekly catechism lessons in Burchwert. Hichtum and Burchwert together make up one congregation.

The only time she gets some time off – and then only so much and not more – is Sunday, in between milkings. But she makes full use of it then by memorizing as many psalms and hymns and Bible verses as possible. And that's when it becomes clear that she's smarter than most. Everyone is amazed how on Sunday evenings she can recite a whole set of new stanzas and Bible passages by heart.

This Ytsje is not reluctant to lay a religious text on someone now and then. Enough to make the farmer and his wife think: "Darn it, who does she think she is to give us a piece of her mind? There we go again – that cheeky young girl slinging a couple of lines from a psalm or hymn in our ears: 'Before my foes Thy mercy show; That Thou dost help me make them know.'"

When after the bitter cold February of 1863 the last snow has finally disappeared, the mail brings three letters especially addressed to Ytsje. The first one is from an uncle who proves to be the writer for her dad Sibbele Wytsma:

Due to the last stage of consumption your Father's weakness has already called him to be bedridden, thence it appears advisable not to come home, however dearly your father would have you with him once more.

The second remaining message is one with a black border around it: Dad's death notice. The third letter comes from the village of Rommerskirchen right beneath Cologne where young Meindert Birdie is earning a good monthly wage as a milker.

Nevertheless the year passes too slowly, I desire more and more intensely to return to my Fatherland, where the first lapwing egg will well-nigh have been found. [...] In view that I am a free man here, I do wish that I, accompanied

by lapwing and godwit, could return to Hichtum, where I
should also very much like to see you, worthy wool-seeker
friend, to ascertain your present condition.

Ytsje, with her religious inclinations, sometimes comes out with the strangest stuff. One day she informs the farmer's wife that a divine mission is awaiting her. "I received the prophecy that I will travel to the New World. America, that is for me the Promised Land; my stay here is but temporary."

The farmer's wife pays little attention, for where would such a half-grown girl get the money to pay for the passage to America? The deceased Sibbele Wytsma could barely afford to pay for a stone on his grave, so not a penny was left to the child, and neither can one buy a ticket out of the farm girl's annual pay of a hundred and twenty-five guilders.

On November 1, 1870, a new farmhand appears in Syswert. He is a tall young man, not an everyday kind of appearance, especially not in Ytsje's eyes. And then the man's name: Hizkia Namminga. This man bears the name of the biblical king Hezekiah. Ytsje thinks: there must be a higher purpose behind this, she's destined to marry this Hizkia, with him she will find the way to the New World. The intensity of Ytsje's faith is rivaled by her flaming passion for this handsome fellow. There is no stopping it now.

Hizkia proves himself an amicable and easy-mannered kind of person. Let's call him pleasant. Well, okay, more like accommodating. As the regular farmhand, he keeps bumping into Ytsje, who in the meantime has become a senior farm maid, everywhere, if not in the milking parlor or barn, then in the haymow or the calf shed. And finally, a bridal suite beneath the rafters, and desire enough to risk the consequences of this blind adventure. That wonder takes place in one of the cruelest winters on record: the winter of 1870-1871.

When the farmer and his wife discover in the spring of 1871 that Ytsje is pregnant by the new farmhand, both are fired that same evening. "That this happened under my own roof," the farmer's wife cries. Ytsje wastes no time; she makes her departure with the words: "Everything that comes to Hizkia and me is controlled by Him."

"Then this too!" the farmer barks. "You are fired!" All of Ytsje's worldly possessions as live-in farm maid fit inside a wheelbarrow, and there's still room for Hizkia's bundle as well. "Mom, we have to get married." Hizkia's confession must've shocked widow Pierkje Namminga-Weima from Easterein. Understandably, because the woman has often warned her boy: "Always use your head, boy, especially when you feel lust trying to get the upper hand. Don't let the middle get control over the two ends." But it hasn't done any good. Isn't the poverty bad enough? As a wedding present she can't give her boy, besides her blessing, more than a set of flannel underwear in which her husband died in the late winter of 1855.

On May 13, 1871, the day has arrived – a civil marriage. It's on a Saturday morning because that's the time when a wedding is cheapest. It costs the young couple a guilder and a half, and their vows. Bride and bridegroom are in luck. *We were married in dry spring weather,* it says in Ytsje's diary, which she begins on May 1.

> *[...] so from now on I am in the eyes of the civil law the wife of Hizkia. [...] On the way back from the city hall my husband found near Sinnema-State five unincubated duck eggs. He spoke to me, this is your well-earned wedding present, Ietje*, you may eat all of them because you still have some growing to do. [...]*

Springtime, wedding season. The week before May 13 we count in the Leeuwarden newspaper more than two hundred family notices

---

* Frisians would typically speak the Frisian language, but write in Dutch. Ietje is the Dutch version of Ytsje.

announcing weddings and wedding anniversaries. And then this recommendation: 'Ready to breed at Jarich Boersma in Friens a pureblood Holstein Bull. Stud fee ƒ 1.50.' And a day or so later in the same paper this advertisement: 'Available, a hardworking farm-worker, knowledgeable about all dairy farm work, as well as a first-rate milker.'

Is Ytsje right? Is all of this controlled? It is the farmer from Syswert who responds. Doesn't the man have a hunch that the advertisement could very well be from Hizkia and Ytsje? Or does the farmer know that and did he have regrets after Rev. Duval Slothouwer confronted him again? How far will the agreeableness of her biblical king stretch? Hizkia reports again to the yard which not long ago he left. All right then, Hizkia is willing to come back only if he will get paid 1.50 more per week. The young couple is able to rent a 'room with bed' for two guilders a week.

While Hizkia already gets homesick when he can no longer see the Hichtum tower, Ytsje talks night and day about America. Time and again her husband lets her know that his dreams do not go beyond having his own milking cows. "Who knows, Ytsje, I might eventually be able to rent the dike berms between Hichtum and the Burchwert corner." That would enable him to have enough to feed four cows, and in addition maybe a couple of working man's cows, that is to say milking goats.

Ytsje is visibly waxing with child; she must be about four months along when she reports as a milker at the Pigskin, the farm of my great-great grandfather and -mother Lieuwe Mensonides and his twenty-two-year-younger IJbeltsje Faber. It earns her a weekly pay of ƒ 2.75. Good pay, though it means that the future dad and mom have to be in their wooden shoes at 3:30 in the morning.

While Hizkia sets out for Syswert, Ytsje takes the old paths through the fields which she first got to know as a little wool-seeker girl. Even in a dense fog she can find the way to the spot where she has to row herself across Kleaster Canal in order to get to Pigskin farm. A one-way trot to the farm takes nearly three quarters of an hour. Milking eight cows and additional chores take about two hours. Assuming that the cows must be milked twice a day, a milker is in harness for about six hours a day. There's a chance that Ytsje succeeds in laying her weekly ƒ 2.50 aside as savings. Each week a little closer to her land of hopes and dreams.

After my great-great grandfather Lieuwe Mensonides passes away, his widow becomes even more generous: Ytsje's wages are increased to ƒ 3.50 per week.

Pencil notes by IJbeltsje – in the margins of Dr. W.C.H. Staring's *The Farmer's Almanack* (December, 1871) – show the following:

> *Hizkia's Ietje is so far along, it looks like she will be delivered of her first child before Christmas, old Pierkje will be her midwife, we have already had six cows calve, so we hope that Ietje will be prezent again by New Year's morning.*

It turns out that IJbeltsje is not far off. It is likely that Ytsje had her first contraction during the evening milking. It's on December 21 after evening milking time that she tramps back home along the hard frozen field paths, beneath a clear sky strewn with stars. Suddenly she realizes that Christmas is approaching. Will it go with her like Mary who was pregnant with God's son, walking every day and barely making it in time to the stable of the inn?

Later she will record the journey from the Pigskin to Hichtum this way:

> *It was such beautiful winter weather, the air carried the sounds so clearly out of the east, which indicates frost, that Hizkia could hear the yard dogs bark all the way from Nijlân.*

When Ytsje made it home, Hizkia, after a long day of work for the farmer, must have finished the milking and feeding of his one cow and couple of goats. You bet, besides his farm labor he has already progressed to being the smallest dairyman of Hichtum.

"Hizkia, it's on the way!" Immediately an alert goes out to the midwife. For that he has to go to his old mother, Pierkje Weima. And thus Ytsje Namminga-Wytsma gives birth on the shortest day of the year 1871 to a healthy boy. It is not likely that the procreator was present at the birth, because giving birth was exclusively for female attendance. Contrary to tradition, the boy is not named after the late grandpa Nammen Namminga, but after Ytsje's early deceased father, Sibbele Wytsma, to whom she had such a loving attachment. Hizkia approves all of it; as far as he's concerned, this will not be their only child. Ytsje is of the same mind: after all, the biblical king Hezekiah had a whole bunch of sons.

At the Pigskin on January 5, a memorandum appears in the margin of Dr. Staring's almanac from great-great grandma IJbeltsje. By then Ytsje is no longer in bed recovering from childbirth; she's very much back to milking.

> *Now that the winter weather is tempering and it is thawing hard and foggy the ice is not to be trusted so that Hizkia's Ietje can walk again through the fields, Jan together with Sjoerd has lain boards for her across Kleaster Canal so that she can be here on time.*

Though Hizkia may be the accommodating kind, time and again he manages to postpone Ytsje's emigration plans. IJbeltje Mensonides-Faber:

> *Ietje is full of emigrating to America while her husband seems more sensible, Hizkia is very fond of Hichtum.*

LIKE KING HEZEKIAH

By the end of the 70s farmhand and small dairyman Namminga has as many children in the front as he has cows at the back of his dwelling. After Sibbele came a Nammele, a Geartsje, and a Lolke. In the back Hizkia has the responsibility for three milking cows, two pigs, and two goats. That means sixteen hours of labor, seven hours of sleep, and an hour of checking on what needs attention. No time to read a paper.

At the Pigskin it's different. The wall of the cattle barn behind the row of cows is plastered with the Leeuwarden newspaper. Purpose: it cuts down on spring cleaning; you need only to soak the papers and peel them off, and the wall is clean. And then there's still another purpose:

> *Unlike our neighbors my husband didn't want to plaster the papers on the wall upside down so that the workers too can stay a little informed about what's going on in the world.*

And a lot was going on. Milker Ytsje must have had her eyes fixed at times on the page with the arrival and departure times of the Holland-America Line. 'America' and 'emigration': those new buzzwords are like music to her ears.

Between the dried-up manure specks she encounters yet another phrase: 'Agricultural crisis.'

In 1879 the economic recession can already be felt in the countryside. Does Ytsje realize that the decline is partly due to the massive export of cheap American grain? Does she understand that the crisis will hurt her household too?

When one morning Hizkia sees his boss, who had been declared bankrupt, hang from the rafters, he, in a manner of speaking, also has a noose around his own neck. The landowner terminates the lease to the widow, and the succeeding renter does not dare to assume the risk of taking on a steady farmhand. That's how one thing leads to another: apparently, terrible cattle disease goes with an agricultural crisis.

The small dairyman from Hichtum is unmercifully reminded of that: all three of his cows die. When the emergency butcher from Burchwert has dragged his last cow from the yard, Hizkia stands behind the old shed weeping.

Grandma IJbeltsje delivers her own commentary:

> *A heavy blow for the young couple, Ietje says that Hizkia*
> *now dawdles over his food, and the man is scrawny as it*
> *is whilst Ietje always stays in fine fettle and positive, some-*
> *times whilst milking she sings together with Sjoerd and*
> *Auck 'Chant through the world God's acts of might' so that*
> *it resounds through the entire milking barn.*

Ytsje sees it as a sign from a higher power. "The Lord our Lord just wants to impress on us that the ocean steamer lies ready to bring us to the land of deliverance."

"But I'm not ready for that yet." The small dairyman, who's become an ordinary farmhand again, has, through all the setbacks, more in common with poor Job than with the self-assured biblical king.

The recession makes widow IJbeltje Mensonides-Faber even thriftier than she already was. Ytsje loses her milking job. Her children will just have to work a little harder now. They become farm hands when they turn twelve.

By 1881 the recession slashes so deep that more than 700 residents from the municipalities of East- and Westdongeradiel, It Bilt, Ferwerderadiel, Barradiel, and Wûnseradiel decide to emigrate. Between 1880 and the onset of WWI in 1914, some 10,000 people from the North-Frisian agricultural region eventually risk the big step[*]. Meanwhile Ytsje runs out of patience. She approaches her oldest son Sibbele who lives away from home as a farmhand: "Son, it's time, we sail under Jesus' protection to America. That is the land of deliverance for people like us. I want you to take the boat to America as our forerunner."

"I'm not ready for that," is Sibbele's response. Sibbele Namminga doesn't want to waste any words on the subject; he wants to go his own way. For his mother there's no solution but to peddle bread for a local baker.

And so Hizkia's Ytsje trudges from door to door with two baskets on a yoke, from Bolsward to Burchwert, from Wommels to Wytmarsum. The yoke of the recession and the discipline of the free market weigh heavily on her shoulders; in one year the number of bread peddlers has more than doubled. Besides, it seems as if there are only Dutch Reformed bakery goods in her basket. Her honey bread may be the best, but the Secessionists, the Mennonites, and the Catholics stick to their own taste.

But Ytsje is not easily defeated. She decides to take a chance on the Reformed farmer with the large family in the hamlet of Pankoeken near Wytmarsum. After an hour and a half of slogging underneath the heavy yoke, she hears: "We stick to our own town; widow Zylstra has already been here." When she comes home, she finds a husband who's struggling with depression.

It's not until the 90s that things begin to look up a bit. The crop prices begin to rise, wages go up, and Hizkia gets a milking job again. Ytsje returns from peddling bread. It's been a hot summer day, and the evening is still very muggy. She's only up to the church when she hears the rhythmic tapping of Hizkia's whetting hammer on the edge of the scythe blade. Apparently he still wants to do some mowing with a sharp scythe. The tap-tap-tap sounds like the

---

[*]   Annemieke Galema: *Frisians to America, 1880-1914.*

beginning of their marriage: allegro moderato. A little later she sees him on the steep bank swinging away in his red flannel undershirt and white long johns. "I have good news," he says. "The heifer has calved, we gained a nice little heifer calf today."

It is the "golden calf." She doesn't come up with this herself, no, it just comes to her. "The golden calf that will lead you and me finally to the land of justice, Hizkia." She wakes her husband up in the middle of the night and tells him that she was shaken awake just now. "Through Him I was shown a moment ago the path to a world without troubles. I have to take Sibbele aside again and present my vision of this night; this time I'll get him to go as our pioneer to America, like the oldest son of King Hezekiah who was sent ahead to the other side of the ocean as quartermaster."

"The ocean." Hizkia is cruelly disturbed out of his sleep. "The ocean, you say it just like it's nothing, but you don't know how much I dread it, those newfangled steamboats forged out of iron that will sink like a brick."

"You have to trust me and the Lord, Hizkia."

"But my dear, the times will get better here too." Hizkia, anxious now, sits up: "We just got a heifer calf, and now this."

Do the times improve? The May 1894 issues of the Leeuwarden newspaper tell us the facts. We see a doubling of the number of construction contracts. Yet another economic farm barometer: J.A. Oosterbaan from Achlum dares to ask three guilders as stud fee for his bull. Not so long ago the purebred bull of Jarich Boersma in Friens did it for half that much. But it's a matter of what one wants to believe or not believe: Ytsje heard that Jetse Feenstra from Allingawier says farewell in the newspaper to all his family, friends, and acquaintances with this announcement: 'We're going to America.'

Ytsje wants to see Sibbele and for the second time impress her will on him. Will it work this time? The giant of a man is no longer a farmhand; he takes one training course after another and wants to become a rural police constable. He's already applied for the vacancy in Huzum.

In his new police uniform he shows up in his Hichtum parents' house, and like a handsome midshipman he stands before his mother in her piebald apron. Hizkia is inclined to look up to his oldest son, but with Ytsje it's different: "You as our first-born, you may not neglect your holy duty, you are to honor your father and mother by supporting them, like the god-fearing sons of the god-fearing King Hezekiah did for their parents. The sons of the king accompanied their parents on the path that God pointed out to them, the first-born in front. And God would keep his hand of protection over Hezekiah's home and family. Look at your mother, Sibbele! Act according to what pleases the Lord our Lord. Boy, don't let this become a day of disgrace, but travel before us as our guide to prepare a place for us in the land where we are awaited."

Sibbele shakes his head and, together with his girlfriend, goes his own way.

Second son Nammen as a second chance? He's more accommodating than his oldest brother, but that doesn't mean his mother quite has him on the other side of the ocean yet. Nammen has lost his heart to farmer's daughter Lysbeth Struiving from Wûns. Lysbeth isn't the type to let anyone tell her what to do. "There's no way I'm going to emigrate before my marriage."

"Why don't you get married, then!" says Mother. Well, that doesn't fall on deaf ears, so they hurriedly get hitched. But when Nammen, now married and all, comes home with Lysbeth, the bride says: "I want to know first if we're able to have children, because when I emigrate I'm doing it for the children."

Mother isn't easily bowled over by one strike, not even by two, instead it seems that she's playing along; before long there's a baby girl. "I want the kids to grow a little older before you get me on the ship to America."

And then it happens that Grandma slams on the brakes herself. Ytsje becomes pregnant by nearly worn-out Grandpa Hizkia. Hichtum is perplexed. Has King Hizkia not proclaimed himself as King Solomon? And doesn't Grandma Ytsje compete with Sarah for the crown here?

"Ytsje thought that she was way past her child-bearing days," Hizkia apologizes. "But you never know of course with Ytsje."

Ytsje does know: "The Lord our Lord had a hand in this. Now that Sibbele refuses to follow the example of the sons of King Hezekiah, He made my womb fruitful once more for a descendant. And we shall name him Jacob."

A couple days after giving birth Ytsje is back, bent over the washtub. And her other half, the farmhand and small dairy farmer Grandpa Hizkia, is back at it too by four o'clock in the morning. In the evenings, near nine o'clock, the old folk hang their outer clothes over the railing of the chair and crawl into the bedstead. Grandma first, as in everything else. And then, between them, the robust baby 'Benjamin' who lets himself doze off to sleep at the still generous breast of the mother and grandmother.

Grandpa looks on and is stirred. "What an abundance of mother milk you have, dear. Where do you get it all!" When the little one has had his fill, it's the big child's turn. "Come on, Hizkia, there's something left for you." And she gives him her breast. "Go ahead and drink, it will give you the strength and the courage to take the big step."

The sweet suckling brings the gray and toothless nursing child back to the beginning of his existence: he is again the child that can't do without Mom; it is as if he wants to return to the womb from which he was born. He refreshes himself from her body and spirit; he smells overripe summer hay, which brings him back to that hot summer day nine months ago. Deep in the hayfield, the sun still high in the southwest, his outer clothing hanging on the gate. He is all by himself to rake the crop of his own small rented plot of land. One quarter acre, not more, but the crop could not be more ample. In the distance, hidden in deep green, a farm here and there. He moves to the edge of the ditch and sees in the surface of the crystal-clear water a steel-blue sky and a silver bird against the heavens. That turns out not to be a bird but his own face with a white beard. To disturb the mirror image he scoops a handful of water from the ditch, and at the same time he hears footsteps in the hay at an angle above him. His wife! There she stands, with her red copper coffee pot and her basket covered with a colorful dishtowel. "I have coffee for you, a piece of calf's leg, and a piece of bread with bacon. You've more than earned it."

"You can't make hay that's riper and more fragrant than this," he mumbles while he lets himself sink down in a pile of hay down the slope of the ditch's embankment. "Smell it once, Ytsje, as ripe, as rich, as spicy as a harvest can get."

"Hizkia, today is the longest and mildest day of this year of the Lord," she begins, as she settles down close to him in the slope of the embankment. "I watched you make hay so nice and all by yourself this afternoon, and all at once I was given the message: here, together, we have to wash our sins and cares away from us."

"Where do you get this, Ytsje; I mean your nice words." He looks at her with admiration, strokes her pinned-up hair with his weathered hand.

"Look," she says, "I've got a little chunk of soft soap and two dishtowels here. I thought, why shouldn't we on this longest day once more get undressed, the ditch is not deep, we get in to soap each other and rinse." While she's saying this she takes her clothes off. "All right," she says when she stands naked in the ditch with the water up to her knees, "now you take your clothes off, then we can soap each other." Hizkia takes a good look around, takes notice how in the distance the farms of Syswert rise up on the horizon. Then he too gets undressed and steps in.

"All right," she says when the foam is rinsed off her body. "Doesn't it make you feel too that we've washed the old land off from us, Hizkia? I think that's how the Song of Songs puts it. Why don't you come here, Hizkia, because our love is like the most wonderful

36

wine, and the sound of your name is still added to that."

And now, so much later in bed with the child between them, there is the sound of her voice again: "Now, Hizkia, you have received what I with all my heart wanted to give you, and it will encourage you to cross the ocean with me. Should our Lolke, like Sibbele, also meet the wrong woman and refuse to go ahead of us, then we still have Geartsje; she's growing up to be a steadfast young woman and I'm sure she will meet the right man, one who will level the path to America for us."

Filled and dreamy with what his wife has offered him, Hizkia begins to dream himself onboard a steamship, loaded with emigrating dairy farmers. Sea and wind begin to rise, the ship heaves as the wind gathers increasingly more force. Will they be all right? The ship begins to list, and then it capsizes. He feels himself pulled toward the bottomless depths. He succeeds in surfacing, but then he has to fight against drowning. All around him at least a hundred pairs of dairy farmer clogs. And in the distance the bells are tolling. Yes, the tower of Hichtum is tolling the emergency bell.

"Ytsje, my clogs!!" With the sweat running down his back, Hizkia wakes up.

"Go back to sleep and trust me and the Lord God."

When early in the morning Hizkia gets back into his own wooden shoes, he hardly remembers the shipwreck of the night. And when sixteen hours later he's pretty much done in and the outer clothes are hanging over the chair again, his wife says: "Yes, we should have Meindert Birdie and Willemke over soon for a maternity visit. I will remind them that the world was created with yet another side to it."

"Birdie sees his savior in Domela Nieuwenhuis the socialist front man." Hizkia can't resist. But Ytsje has the liturgy for the visit firmly in place. "I'm sure I can make Birdie understand that his surrogate shepherd of a Domela doesn't have the guts to go along to America, but our Lord God surely will go with us."

Meindert Birdie in the meantime has grown way beyond the dreaming child who sings along with the tunes of the bird kingdom. It is as if the hard times have turned him into a rebellious, at times disturbed, man. Rebellious on account of all the injustice in society, disturbed because he found out that as a small outdoorsman you can't be really free when at the same time needing to make ends meet for a family. That's why Meindert often had to make himself available as a laborer in spots where he found little freedom, equality, and brotherhood.

In the 70s he thought that he had found his land of opportunity in the German Ruhr District. He forged ahead and became head farmhand on a large dairy farm. To get to Germany didn't require crossing an ocean. Besides that, his Willemke van Zandbergen, whom he couldn't do a week without, went along. But even though he made almost twice as much as he slaved for in Hichtum, Birdie was back in Hichtum before egg-hunting season, just to feel as free as a bird for that brief time.

Just outside the village he was able to rent a comfortable small townhouse on the Harlingen Canal. Included were the fishing rights for a part of the Harlingen Canal and the Lollum Canal. There in the open country he could smell freedom. And the view was terrific. That lasted till the day a waste disposal pram appeared. At a distance of less than thirty yards from the house the municipality of Wûnseradiel began to dump the human waste of six villages.

After the first stormy northwester Meindert and Willemke had their windows coated with feces. The unobstructed view – gone; the smell of freedom – gone. Meindert feels himself insulted, and all the more so when no one in the municipality is willing to give his objections a hearing. The next day Meindert and Willemke find themselves once again packing up their furniture. Better to move to the meager little apartment that leans old and wearily against the Hichtum terp. On top of that, with the move, Meindert loses his fishing rights.

On the authority of the mayor, the police appear at his door. With a summons. He is charged with three days of illegal fishing. Yes, indeed, he has to make his appearance. Upset, he walks across the fields to Wytmarsum to explain to the bigwigs that he acted in good faith.

It turns into a confrontation with Mayor Carl W.T. Visser. Meindert discovers that the mayor transferred the fishing permit for a part of the Harlingen and Lollum Canal to the skipper of the new shit pram. "But you cannot do that without letting me know!" When the magistrate snaps at him, Meindert barks back: "I won't let anyone humiliate my wife and children, and especially not a mayor."

Visser can't believe his ears. "You give a big mouth to the mayor?"

Meindert Birdie loses it and hollers that he refuses to be a citizen for one more second under such a tyrant. "I'll move to Hinnaarderadiel, or to Baarderadiel, or to Wymbritseradiel." Carl W.T. Visser, one of the most notorious bullies that the Frisian guild of mayors has ever produced, is in his element. "What? I'm going to smear you with a criminal record so that you will not be admitted as a resident anywhere anymore. And you will never again receive a permit; not to fish in inland waterways, not to catch birds, or to mow the banks. Birdie, there's nowhere for you to turn anymore, not to other municipalities, not to Holland, not to Germany, not to America – you're wingless, Birdie."

When moments later he stands outside on shaky legs, he is completely torn up. Nearly in a panic. The last fragment of freedom has been taken from him. On the way home he meets his old wool-seeker friend Ytsje beneath the yoke of her breadbasket. "What all are you telling me? It's going to turn out all right, man. I will ask the minister to pin the mayor's ears back with Proverbs 21 verse 13: 'If a man shuts his ear to the cry of the poor, he too will cry out and not be answered.' Come over Saturday evening with Willemke for a maternity visit; that will encourage you and the wife. I can tell you right now that there's still another world with a better government waiting for us."

Meindert and Willemke are welcomed in the small living room not only by the parents of the youngest resident of Hichtum. There's another, silent, witness: the stuffed curlew which Hizkia and Ytsje received from the Boorsmas as a wedding present. The bird is really too big for the small mantelpiece. "Birdie, listen to me," Ytsje begins. "I understand from Mrs. Mensonides that the mayor can't touch you. You can be and go wherever you want to."

After coffee the men enjoy an undiluted gin. Ytsje thinks: the men better do their own sousing first. Both of the ladies will do fine with one cupful of raisins in brandy wine. The men start to talk louder, while the women go down to whispering about the symptoms and side effects of being of the female gender.

Manhood is no picnic either, they're talking about the weather and the diseases of the animal kingdom, till they can no longer stand the gloom of the present times and escape to the past. Not that the past was better, but at least poverty didn't get the best of them.

The host does what he's not usually so good at doing: he pours, and spills.

"Cheers, Meindert!"

"To your health, Hizkia."

"Birdie..." Hizkia starts whispering. "You pressed something on my heart some time ago, and you were right: we can't take our soul along across the wide ocean."

Meindert leans with his best ear toward his friend and whispers back: "Your wife wants to leave here in the worst way but you're hanging back."

"Leaving, that's no longer necessary." Hizkia boldens. "Our children are already better off than we were."

"Wait a minute," cries Meindert, "each generation a few pennies ahead, that's not getting us anywhere. Hiz, you're going with me next Saturday night to Easterlittens to listen to a certain Domela Nieuwenhuis. Small dairymen and laborers can get in free. Domela is a man of insight."

Ytsje is all ears. "There is only one savior, Meindert! You and I, we sang it together as children: 'Valiant with God on our side, we turn our eyes to the unknown land.'"

"I'm done singing!" Meindert Boorsma leans forward in his chair. Does he want to go home? No, he's staring at the stuffed curlew on the mantelpiece.

Hizkia succeeds in pouring one more time. Far in the distance he hears the humming of female voices, it's about stuffed animals that serve only as dust catchers. And then the word 'America' is dropped.

"Birdie!"

"Go ahead."

"A couple of drinks and I'm deaf. Not drunk, but just deaf."

Meindert looks at his friend and together they flee to the past as fast as they can. "You seeded Ytsje's garden in Syswert when I sat on the other side of Kleaster Canal in the cold behind my plover hide-out. There I called and serenaded the plovers with one song, just like you called and serenaded your wife with one song. A rustling cloud of birds came toward me, a cloud filled with life. A bright lapwing stood on my seesaw, a dang plucky decoy bird, and then it hopped up to wave at the flight. And then, at the right moment, I tugged at the pull line. A net full of life. And the same for the curlew. Here, the same for me, here…"

"And now," stammers Hizkia while he reaches with one shaky hand for the empty bottle and with the other points to the mantelpiece, "now the curlew is dead."

Meindert listens with wet eyes. "Our curlew, he isn't a shadow anymore of what he was in the beginning of our marriage. The luster of life no longer lies over it."

When just before midnight the guests have left, the curlew on the mantelpiece has disappeared. "Just take it with you," Ytsje had ordered.

By the time that Hizkia drops in bed beside his wife, Meindert in the presence of Willemke brings the curlew to the cemetery, to the

41

place where they've planned to have their grave. It is right behind the church, not far from the bricked-up window and the cistern. "Here is our place," he says in his short funeral oration. "The comfort bird has gone before us."

To America

It's around seven in the evening in May 1905 when someone's at the door. A young man. Did Ytsje really go so far as to respond to that small ad in Hepkema's paper*? A 'decent milk hauler' asked for a place to board in the Bolsward area. Yes, they had become subscribers to the paper, and Mother didn't skip a word. 'A decent milk hauler,' she had said aloud while reading. Now that the oldest boys were out of the house, there was room for 'a tame sheep.' Where is the ambitious young man who dares to cross the ocean with daughter Geartsje to take up quarters on the other side?

A boarder makes his appearance. But will that be the one? Geartsje, sent by Mother to the door, opens the door slightly at first, then wide. Briefly she is speechless.

"Douwe Hiemstra!"

"Come on in."

She shakes hands with him but forgets to introduce herself. She feels the firmness of his handshake. And callouses. This could well be the milk hauler.

"I'm Hizkia and Ytsje's Geartsje," she hears herself say. The old man in the arm chair has the appearance of an old patriarch with his snow-white hair and beard, but it doesn't take the guest long to realize who's the one that waves the scepter. Mother! Dad uses the same chewing tobacco Douwe is addicted to – *De Jong* from Joure.

"And how old is Douwe," the wife wants to know.

"Almost twenty-two, Mrs. Namminga."

"As if ordained, Douwe is not much older than our Geartsje!"

After he's asked, Douwe, who is indeed looking for a boarding

---

* A regional newspaper, *Nieuwsblad van Friesland*, but often called Hepkema's paper after its editor.

place, tells where he's from. He is a Penjumer. Penjum was once labeled by Ytsje as red, or socialist-leaning. A handful of big crop farmers, a potato- and grain merchant, some ten dairymen, an army of casual laborers.

"From what kind of a family, Mrs. Namminga?"

There were eleven children, and they realized that most of the work had to be found outside the Penjum Collar*. And now he's able to land an excellent milk route for the Bolsward KNM milk factory.

"Eventually have some of my own cows, is what I was thinking."

"Room and board." Mrs. Namminga doesn't want to skirt around the issue anymore. She'd been thinking of four and a half guilders a week. Bed, meals, laundry – everything included.

"Let's go with that." Douwe had really regarded his mission a success already at the door. Who knows, there could be more included than room and board.

"Does Douwe first want to see his bed, maybe? Let me tell you right now that we sleep on buckwheat shells here and not simply on straw. Buckwheat is good for rheumatism." The new boarding house mistress leads the lodger up the ladder to the cramped little loft. "It is ample size, a three-quarter bed."

"This will be fine, Mrs. Namminga." One would think that nothing fazes this sturdy young man. "You can, so to speak, join us right away, Douwe."

"Tomorrow night around this time I'll be blowing in, Mrs. Namminga."

On the first Monday morning after Douwe's arrival in Hichtum, long modern snow-white underpants dance in the spring breeze right next to Geartsje's flesh-colored panties.

"Oh gosh, this is going to be trouble," Meindert Birdie calls out right after ringing the noon hour bells as he walks down the church

---

*   The Penjum Collar is a circular dike around the village of Penjum, protecting it from the sea.

path. "Watch out, Geartsje girl, all you need is a clothes pin to let go and the new boarder has you pregnant with child."

Foresight? Douwe and Geartsje fall hard for each other. Plenty of reason for Ytsje to acquaint Douwe with the Promised Land. The words "preparing the way" are dropped in conversation.

"You mean emigration. That seems quite something to me." Douwe smiles and sounds totally disinterested. Ytsje senses that she won't easily turn him on to America.

As soon as he stretches his legs out under the table, his socks go in search of Geartsje's. Or he turns to the mild man who, if all goes well, will become his father-in-law. And he also gets along fine with his future brothers-in-law. He's realized early on: he'll have to take the mother in with the bargain.

Not quite a half year after Douwe came in the back door, he leaves with Geartsje through the front door. On Saturday morning, May 20, 1905, they marry in Wytmarsum. And it's high time. They quickly rent a room in the neighborhood.

In the cruel cold of February 1906, after a long and difficult delivery, Geartsje gives birth to twin boys: Jabik, named after Douwe's father, and Hizkia. The anxiety is plainly written on the faces of Ytsje and the midwife from Burchwert; the babies look like they're in trouble. Douwe, in terrible weather, hurries through high snow drifts to Bolsward to fetch a doctor.

The doctor says that he'll be in Hichtum inside of an hour, but three hours later he's still not there. And not even when a neighbor boy is sent to the city with an urgent written request to come at once. And all this time the wind and the snow do not let up. After a day and a night filled with worry and empty promises from the doctor, both boys die. Geartsje, more reserved than her mother, demonstrates that she – in spite of all the sorrow – is a strong and well-grounded woman. Her husband, however, doesn't know where to turn.

Douwe, who has recently become Hichtum's gravedigger, feels the hand of his new friend Johannes, son of Meindert and Willemke,

45

on his shoulder. "Give me the spade, let me do this sad duty for you, and I'll take your milk route for you too. You stay with Geartsje."

It's a half year later when an informational evening is held in Bolsward about emigration to America. "This is where all of us need to go." Ytsje succeeds in taking Douwe and Geartsje, her son Nammen with his Lysbeth Struiving, and her still single son Lolke along. Douwe even gets his peer Johannes Boorsma to join. "No, Hizkia doesn't feel up to it, he'd rather stay at home."

The speaker is Mr. Albert Kuipers, a prominent farmer and land broker in southeast South Dakota. Kuipers introduces himself as the emigrant who's become a roaring success on the other side of the pond. He opens the gathering with prayer. "Because no matter where we are in the world, not only the same sun shines on us but the same God is in control."

"Let's get down to business!" The speaker forges ahead. "In the beautiful state of South Dakota there's a world of excellent farmland available for everyone who's not afraid of work. You can pick it up all over for a song." An image emerges of a huge herd of cattle, grazing in a deep green hilly landscape. "Well, not far from my farm and those of my own boys who've already become independent farmers, runs the mighty Missouri River, which makes it a very fertile area, and so is our whole Bonhomme district."

What appeals to some of those present, and certainly to Ytsje too: "For us believers there's a rich church life, and besides that there's even a lively Frisian society. You bet, good Frisians, we took our language with us even though we have to learn English in addition. But that's normal."

It's time for questions. "Mr. Speaker, I expect an honest answer to my question." Johannes Boorsma introduces himself as the son of Meindert Birdie from Hichtum. "I do have adventure in me, but I don't care much for all the nice talk from land brokers and shipping agents."

"You had a question?" Kuipers sounds quite irritated.

"Don't the farmers in South Dakota suffer pretty badly from dry summers now and then? Aren't the winters there often unbearably cold? And not so many years ago, weren't thousands of Indians massacred after the colonists stole all their land? Tell us everything, Kuipers!"

Kuipers tries hard to stay calm, and that gives Johannes another chance to ask a question. "I would like to know if this man covered his own round trip ticket to and from Friesland. Kuipers! Are you standing before us speechifying as someone paid by the Royal Dutch Steamship Company? Are you a farmer only or also a travel agent and land broker?"

The speaker begins to stutter his denials, so that Johannes can finish him off: "People, don't let anybody mess with your heads, what we're hearing here is nothing but gospel, syrup and honey. You can also earn good money in the German dairies, you can travel from Leeuwarden to Cologne by train in one day, but even there along Ruhr and Rhine it's not rice and raisins every day. Except that from Germany you can go home for a few days for the egg hunt or to celebrate the Bolsward Fair."

Furious, Ytsje Namminga-Wytsma rises from her chair. "Meindert Birdie's Johannes leans toward the socialists!" Whatever is said after that makes little difference, the information evening has been derailed.

When they get home, Hizkia has something to share too: "Something is messed up, I have the bank-mower's cross." In other words, the man has a hernia, most likely incurred by scythe-mowing the deep and steep dike banks. "I've been running around with it for a while, but I dreaded to tell you about it."

"I haven't noticed anything unusual lately."

"When I lie down the hernia slips back inside. Have a look." After her husband has dropped both pairs of pants, Ytsje observes the bulging tissue.

"They won't want this man in America in this condition." Hizkia says it with a sigh of relief.

Ytsje sits down, thinks for a moment, then says: "When King Hezekiah lived the way God wanted him to, all he needed to do was put a fig cake on his growth and his problem disappeared!"

But the problem did not disappear; the hernia is still there on May 13, 1906, the day that Hizkia and Ytsje Wytsma have their 35th wedding anniversary. The children see to it that Bolsward photographer Jacob de Vries comes to immortalize the couple on a glass plate negative. On the picture we see the couple stand next to their house in front of the open barn door, he smiling slightly, she more stern. An old bride and bridegroom in black, both in black wooden shoes that gleam in the spring's sun. Hizkia's snow-white beard stands out in bright contrast to his black Sunday cap. She wears her white crochet hat with a loop in the string right underneath her prominent chin. We see two sunken mouths which tell us that both are missing most of their teeth. His fine, bony hands look puny compared to her large, strong, milker's hands. Is it out of affection that his arm touches her left arm, or is he just leaning toward her because he mowed himself into a hernia?

A good four months later, on Friday September 21, 1906, Hizkia Nammens Namminga passes away. The cause could have been a strangulated hernia. When the immediate family gathers in the mortuary in Hichtum on Saturday September 22, the oldest son, Sibbele, looks his mom straight in the eyes when he says: "It was out of respect for my dad that I didn't go to America as quartermaster. Only in Hichtum could this man be happy." Brothers, sisters, son-in-law and daughters-in-law receive his words with emotion and approval.

It is the third son who, not much later, is the first to board the ship to New York. As a bachelor he wants to prepare the way for those to follow. It appears that he's already been in correspondence with farmers in South Dakota. There in Bonhomme they have had a decent summer. Before Lolke says his goodbyes, he promises Douwe Hiemstra to keep the home front well informed of the conditions in the Dakotas.

It is four months later. Douwe and Geartsje are not very impressed by what Lolke writes. From his letters they can only conclude that it's a matter of hoping for better times.

Almost a year later, February 29, 1908. Douwe and Geartsje begin to thrive thanks to their own milk production plus the milk hauling business. They request and receive a building permit in Hichtum for 'a house with a cow barn.' In the municipal archives of Wûnseradiel there's proof that they didn't have to wait long. On 19 December of the same year Douwe also asks for a permit 'to build a shed for fattening pigs and for two more cows.'

But then a letter arrives in late summer of 1909 from Springfield, SD.

> [...] I bought a large piece of prime land for but a few dollars which I had saved up, so the situation here is beginning to look really really good. [...]

In Hichtum the youngest son, Jacob, meanwhile almost grown up, will not be held back anymore and embarks with his girlfriend Rinskje Steffen-Bruinsma from Easterein. Rinskje already has a couple of brothers in South Dakota. In his first letter, sent upon arrival at Ellis Island in New York, Jacob writes:

> [...] After a talk with the minister, we were advised to get married quickly.

Beginning of December 1910. Douwe and Geartsje get their act together and sell their small but successful dairy to farmhand Poortinga from Burchwert. At that point Ytsje realizes that there's only one thing that can cause a hitch in the plans: a letter with bad news from Lolke or Jacob. The old rascal makes a deal with the mailman that all letters from America will be delivered to her personally and privately.

49

The day of departure has been set: February 15, 1911. Ytsje manages to get son Nammen to publicize this happy fact to the whole Hichtum area. The next day everyone has heard: Ytsje is getting her way: she will travel under His care to the New World. Accompanying her will be Nammen, his wife Lysbeth Struiving with their five children, and daughter Geartsje with her husband Douwe Hiemstra and their three small children. On the night of 16 to 17 February the steamship Noordam will be ready for sailing – regardless of weather.

In a note dated February 15, addressed to Johannes Boorsma (who at the time apparently had temporary work in the Zaan region), his father Meindert Boorsma writes, also in the name of mother Willemke:

> [...] Very early this morning we saw Ietje with her adult
> Children and Grandchildren who still live here go to the
> cemetery. Sibbele was there too to say goodbye. They all
> wanted to visit Hizkia's Grave one more time, and the
> Grave of Douwe and Geertje's Twins. [...] Last night Ietje
> was over to say Goodbye and asked me if I would still pull
> her last two lower teeth and three Upper teeth, for she had
> trouble with caries, and hoped to arrive in America without
> that annoyance, which I did in the shed with the Pincers.

It is damp and cold, the 15th of February. Ytsje stands in the cemetery, her descendants crowded around her. The gusty southwest wind sweeps through the bare treetops. The group stops by Hizkia's simple stone, then moves a bit later to the north side of the church where the grave of Douwe and Geartsje's twin boys is. They stand there motionless, as if they want to absorb forever the names chiseled in the hard stone. Then the family – Grandma in front – leaves the old terp. At the end of the church cemetery path Ytsje stops for a moment and then steps, her head held high, onto the road to her land of deliverance.

In Bolsward four large shipping crates and as many heavy wooden suitcases are onboard of the small steamboat which will bring the Nammingas and Hiemstras to Harlingen. It is not clear why water transport was chosen over a train trip from Leeuwarden. Did Ytsje want to add some style to their farewell? The Harlingen Canal circles around the church at a distance of hardly twenty yards, so she could almost make a half-turn around the church and tower. As a last farewell to the living and the dead.

I WANT TO LIVE

The steam engine begins to slow down, huffing and puffing while sliding past a side street, another side street, and a square with a bronze war hero on top of a horse. A bright clearing sets the train car in flashing sunlight, till the shade of the covered railroad station ends it. *Hauptbahnhof Essen*, Germany. With the address of the agent in his head, Johannes Meinderts Boorsma walks out of the station. On the square he asks somebody which direction he should take to get to the village of Frillendorf. That way, points the informer. Johannes swings his kit bag over his shoulder and takes off. A two-hour walk at most, milker agent R. de Jong had written. His office is on the Burggrafenstrasse 311.

The evening before he left he had a run-in with his dad. Bad words were spoken; Johannes has a hard time getting past those; they keep bothering him.

"You like to make it sound good, but can you make it all come true?" That's how it had started. The gist of it was that the old man would rather see him get a job in the Zaan region, or even closer by, in Friesland.

"I don't want to be like you, just trying to make ends meet." Apparently those words fell out too harshly.

"Well, well!"

"Let me say it once more: I will no longer let anyone here walk all over me, not a farmer or anybody else, and I'm no longer going to let those damn meadowland birds call me back."

And then it went all wrong. The old man got up, and then, livid, sank back into the chair.

"You hurt your dad," his mother said. "Son, why is your barometer always set to storm?"

"I don't want to say anything bad about Dad, but all his life he has allowed himself to be driven into a corner. That's not going to

52

happen to me. I want to be free, I want to live!"

Dad, his voice shaking: "Oh sure! You're going to live like a hero while I live like a duffer." A father in tears, a mother trying in vain to calm the storm. He remembers that he ran outside and through the window saw the old man sitting in the house, his back turned to the outside world. Mother brought her son to the small gate by the road. "Son, wherever you go, weigh your words." The mother and the son, who dearly love each other, shake hands, while the father has his back turned against the evil world.

Isn't there a reason, then, to do things differently than Dad? Hadn't there always been unrest in his dad's life? How often didn't he and his brother and sisters on yet another school playground have to fight their way in to belong? In Burchwert, Kûbaard, Lollum, several times in the Ruhr area – ever and always from school to school. And Dad always in search of what didn't exist, at least not for him: Freedom. How often didn't Mom have to wrap up her simple dishes in sheets, aprons, and dishtowels when they once again had to make a move. What the poor dear had in furniture could easily fit in a fishing boat.

Dad. My dad. He felt himself tethered to his birthplace which he seemingly hated and loved at the same time. And always longing for a better place. But at the same time afraid that he couldn't do without that damn tough terp, the terp on which he was born and where he apparently wanted to be buried. The real fate of Meindert Birdie was that he had been born without wings; he had always talked and sung with the birds, even flew along with them a bit. But he caught on that he lacked wings. What remained was only an anchor that he dropped here, then there. "Look, there we have Meindert Birdie with wife and children, hauling in his anchor and moving his boat again."

He had helped his dad to clean the human excrement from the windows on the Hemertertille. Human excrement, including that of the mayor, which stank of injustice. "They've been shitting on us long enough here, let's go!" The very same day they moved to a room in a row house. A ladder to a loft, a makeshift bed with its head-end almost touching the bare roof tiles. The smell of sparrow and starling nests.

Outside, one outhouse for four households, inside only cardboard between the marriage beds of 'the Birdies' and 'the Lumps' – those were the Zonderlands. He could hear Sake and Kee Zonderland moan as if they were in agony. "Oh Sake, careful, careful." Did he soon have to moan along in this miserable world? What do you want to do, Johannes Boorsma? Live in fear all your life, or live?

The farmers alone of Hichtum, Burchwert, and Hartwert made him want to leave. No, just the priggish Jan Lieuwes Mensonides of the Pigskin: "What? Two hundred and fifty guilders is not enough for you? Are you really one of Meindert and Willemke's with that big mouth of yours?" Meindert and Willemke's Johannes was close to knocking the farmer to the ground.

"Get out of here, I don't want you in my yard anymore."

Johannes, on the way to Frillendorf. A young man with a good build, smooth-shaven, mustache neatly trimmed. His deep-set blue-gray eyes don't sparkle, they glimmer and that gives him a mysterious appearance. On the way to the milking job he takes note of everything new around him: the people and their language, the tune of the church bells, the sound of the automobile; it is the song of the present. This adventure is relaxation and liberation at the same time.

He passes a young woman. Oh dear, this is not a girl anymore. When he turns around to look, she turns her head at the same time. And then she disappears around the corner. At an intersection he addresses an older man. Does this road go to Frillendorf? *Jawohl*, if he keeps going in that direction he'll get there in three hours or so. What? Middleman De Jong was talking about a "two-hour walk at most." He walks a ways with the man, searches for words, and says in broken German:

"I want to live!"

"Ja, ja," the man who will soon head in a different direction laughs.

54

"It is live or be lived."

He sees a really cute girl on a bike, her breasts self-consciously thrust forward, her rump enticingly rearward. Between Hichtum and Bolsward he's met a lot of bicyclists, but never such a beautiful woman. Here the most wonderful secret touches the saddle. Johannes sizzles. Life awaits him here. His best friend, Douwe Hiemstra, has let himself be persuaded by old Ytsje and is on the way with the Nammingas to America, but there's something to be accomplished here too. On the way to Frillendorf he counts eighteen factory chimneys. Yes, the Germans have the right idea: not all their eggs in one basket; cows and cannons.

It's nearly seven o'clock in the evening when he rings the bell at Burggrafenstrasse 311. "Mr. de Jong?" He may come in. An old housekeeper explains that De Jong is not home. "But Mr. de Jong was going to be home all day."

"Sorry, Mr. Boorsma." Maybe mister will be home tomorrow.

He looks around; in the hallway a door is ajar, and there he notices 'The Hepkema' and the contact paper for at least five-hundred Frisian milkers in Germany. In the blink of an eye he tears the paper from the table and takes off with it. While walking he scours the help-wanted page and reads that the widow Steinfarz, Gerlingstrasse 28, asks for a milker. He finds out that it is about a half-hour walk.

It's close to eight o'clock when he sits at widow Helga Steinfarz's table behind a hot meal on a large plate. Next to the plate a bottle of beer, across from him the widow. A young widow; she's still good-looking. He feels that she likes him; she even keeps looking at him when she goes into the cellar to fetch another bottle of beer. "You sure are a handsome man, Johannes."

Gosh. "Live and be lived." Stay calm, Johannes, don't gulp. The widow might hear his heart pounding. The fried pig's leg is licked clean; she goes up the stairs ahead of him, slowly and silently. "The bed."

While she undresses, she exclaims that his mustache is fuller and nicer than that of Kaiser Wilhelm. "Hey, don't be afraid, man!" Johannes wants to live and now he's being lived as well.

After a week he's had enough of the widow. The gulps are too big. "No, Mrs. Steinfarz," he says when leaving; she doesn't have to settle with him for the last three days. She's paid him enough. Away. Another place. But where? He'll figure that out.

He now finds agent De Jong at home, he's offered a subscription to 'The Hepkema,' and that's how he finds another place.

What Johannes experiences and what inspires him he records frankly in his newly acquired Hohenzollern diary. He makes one girl after another crazy about him. On the inside of the hard cover he pastes the German spelling rules: Rules of the New Spelling 1910. His entries indicate that he indeed experiences a lot. And he realizes that living begins with breathing and learning the language. After a couple of weeks he writes all nouns with a capital letter even in Dutch*. Later he finds out that his dad as a milker had the same habit. "My father in essence also wanted to live!"

> *Esteemed parents, I left Widow Steinferz Saturday Evening already, for after a Week I had mostly had enough and now I understand that Agent S. Speerstra in Neuss has a good Job for me. Here the Winter is past while the real Spring still has to arrive. Did Dad see and hear the first Lapwings already? Here I have seen only three Pairs, and not a single Godwit.*

A few days later a subsequent message arrives in Hichtum:

> *First I want to thank Dad from the Bottom of my Heart that he, without my initial Notice, stuffed his most precious Lapwing Whistle in my Workpants. When I pulled on my*

---

* German spelling requires all nouns to capitalized, Dutch does not.

Pants on Sunday, I found it. Now maybe I will miss the Call of the Lapwing somewhat less. I am still doing my Best to stick it out here till August, for the Pay is good, and now and then I also enjoy a lively Courtship."

On Sunday evening, August 11, 1912, Johannes is at the door of his old parents in Hichtum.

"Dad is waiting for you, boy," his mom whispers. "He's close to the end."

Meindert Birdie's last anchoring place is even smaller than Johannes had dreamed. Outside the day is ending, inside it's already mostly dark. Dad's empty chair is in the same place as when he left home: with its back toward the evil outside world. Between the two doors of the bedstead the Black Forest cuckoo clock, which the old man once came home with for the great love of his life from his first milking job in Ebersfelz, has stopped. A black cloth, in which Mom had carried her dishes, covers the mirror.

"Here is Johannes," his mother whispers while she opens the bedstead doors a bit wider to let in some light.

"Dad!" Two dull eyes that light up and fasten on the son. He reaches out to his son with what once was the iron-strong fist of Meindert Birdie and now it seems as if the son is holding all of his dad in that one hand.

A day later, on Monday, August 12, 1912, Meindert Boorsma, age 63, dies. Laid out with his hands folded on his chest, and hidden in those hands the thing with which he had serenaded his longing for the Better Land. Johannes has brought the bird whistle back home with him from Germany. "It belongs with Dad on his last journey, it is the mirror of his soul."

A Shipful of Hope

How long has she been onboard? When exactly did she land in this stinking stomach of the SS Noordam? Today? Yesterday? Geartsje Hiemstra-Namminga feels trapped in a haunted no-man's-land where chaos and confusion reign. And where in heaven's name is her husband? A little while ago she heard Douwe's voice. "Take it easy, dearie." And now he's gone. It is ghostly dark; there are only shadows and strange voices.

She hears the blast of the ship's horn. The 12,000-ton ocean steamer is leaving the dock. Her stomach churns, then it turns. A ship loaded with uncertainty and hope. More than a thousand men, women and children of a hundred different kinds and who knows how many languages. Torn loose from their roots. One can hear the language of the helpless mother of the Polish Jewish boy Peche Schajewitz, who the night before was born almost literally at the last minute in Rotterdam. And there is the language of Grandma Ytsje Namminga-Wytsma from Hichtum. Peche, the youngest passenger, Grandma Ytsje perhaps the oldest. They're saying that the boat will make a stop in Northern France. Or were they there already?

"Where were you?" Douwe is back.

"The men are not allowed to come to the women's section, didn't I tell you that?" A hundred voices mingle.

"It's as if we are sailing to Babylon." Grandma is there too, but where exactly? Oh, this must be her place, in the lower berth. Still wearing her overclothes. "I was thinking, I better get some sleep now, once we're on the ocean it won't be so easy." Grandma Ytsje is in safe hands, nothing will happen to her.

"Douwe, take care of the kids a minute," says Geartsje, "I have to go after the diapers, almost all my diapers have been stolen." But Douwe has left already.

"Who has my diapers? They were here a minute ago."

"Aw, bitch, why don't you bugger off!" A few berths down the commotion of a real battle-ax, everywhere the crying of children. Why aren't the men allowed to help their women put the kids to bed?

Geartsje's three fall asleep at last: Jacob four years old, Ytsje two, and Hizkia eight months.

And there's Douwe again, now accompanied by a guard. He whispers that she shouldn't get so upset. "Of course you're rattled, there's a lot weighing on you, but there's a remedy for that: go with me up to deck for a bit, feel the wind in your hair, the guard will have to go too. Come, honey, we can sight land here one more time." Though she's feeling awful, she goes with him.

The first dry snowflakes whip into them as in a storm, a little while later a grayish curtain is closed around them. "There is no land in sight anymore," she declares. She hesitantly lets him take her to the railing. Deep below them, like a passing foaming monster, the ocean. She vomits into it.

Hours later she lies in bed with eyes wide open staring into the darkness. It had been tense, it seemed like a race to be the first to board. Wondering how it all turned out for that couple, Sake and Tryntsje Bylsma, and their lost passage papers. Did they make it onboard or were they sent back to Sint-Anne? Back... there's no way back now. Does Douwe have all the papers in order? What noise is that? Is that a rain shower with a rising wind, or is it still the melancholy violin of that Polish beggar Dobkiewicz? No, the racket comes from one of the children's berths, it must be the cries from that tyke of Aaltsje Oost from Hoarnstersweach, the mom who's still a child herself. She'd forgotten the name of the state where the child's father was waiting for her.

Some more hours later, deep in the nausea-inducing stomach of the steamship, Geartjse Hiemstra-Namminga stumbles around with three whining kids. They are wet and dirty, and the lost diapers have not re-surfaced.

"The little fella is asking for the breast." Grandma is awake and in command again. "Mom, I feel like I don't have a drop of milk, I'm dry."

"No milk left? I've never had that happen." The old lady has a way of hurting her daughter from time to time.

What are they hollering now? Mealtime?

"Oh, no!"

"Yes, it's time to eat, you need to eat well." All right then, finding your way through long corridors and up high stairs. There is the dining room for the lower class.

"You've never had it this good," Grandma opines.

"This looks like it's a bit American," crows her son Nammen. "And I've met a lot of Frisians already, I think it's not a bad idea to get to know as many of your own people as possible. We Frisians have to keep each other in view, then we can find a lot of support from each other in a strange place. We have to get along well with the neighbors."

To judge from his color, Douwe isn't feeling too well, but it's clear he doesn't want to own up to it: "There's Jabik and Albertsje de Jong from Hurdegaryp. Five kids, the oldest not yet ten."

"They are going to New Jersey," Nammen adds, "that's a half-day travel from the Dakotas." He had had trouble with their papers but remained as calm as an old shoe. When things looked really grim, a clerk discovered that they had misspelled his name: Namen Nau-nuiuga. That's why he was first classified with the Hungarians.

"Dirty people." That was Grandma's take. "Petroleum, that's good for pests. In America they have good petroleum."

Nammen has made his own list of Frisian passengers. That's how he got acquainted with Sytske van der Veen from Feanwâlden. "With four kids under ten she's traveling to her husband in… those darn American names are hard to remember, but I understand that their state is not so far from the Dakotas. Do you hear that, Douwe? We won't be alone in America! And there's a Johannes Sietsma and Bouke van der Wint, both from Eanjum. And a Harke Woudwijk

60

from Ljussens, a Wybrand and Aaltsje Jongsma from Ikkerwâld, a Leendert Woudstra from Nijlân. It's possible that I've stood cleaning plants out of ditches with Leendert's brother along Sheeps Lane below Nijlân. I also met the Bosmas and the Van der Meulens. I asked everyone 'How do you write your name,' and it's all clear. There were also a Sjaarda, a Katsma, a Landstra. And a man from Skalsum talked to me, a Piter Breuker. That was when we were still docked in Rotterdam. Piter when he said goodbye to his mom told her that he wanted to become filthy rich before they would see him back in Skalsum. 'Then you better get rich fast,' his mom said. And while I was talking with Piter we saw two fat rats step onboard. They marched over the mooring coils and through the hawse-holes into the ship, so I said: 'Those don't have to buy a ticket.' Piter said, 'Nammen, those two rats are boarding as bride and bridegroom and will arrive in New York with a bunch of kids.' And I say to Piter…"

"Nammen, I want to keep the conversation decent on this trip." Grandma, her hands already folded, retakes control. "Let's pray." When her Amen ends it, Nammen resumes: "There's another man who is going to take the train from New York to Canada, and I think that's closer than the Dakotas."

"Canada is the heart of America," Grandma offers.

Later in the evening there are signs everywhere of the increasing wind. Geartsje unloads her stomach again. "The wind is hitting the ship sideways," the men determine. "A strong wind."

"The Lord will protect us and take care of us." And with those words Grandma is going to go to sleep, trying again to get a head start on her rest. Douwe and Nammen have been upstairs and come back with the news that an icy cold winter wind together with splashing water clouds chased all the fortune seekers from the upper deck.

On the morning of February 25, all hell breaks loose. High seas, a struggling ship. And the rumor is that the worst is still to come.

A frantic ocean appears intent on humiliating the Noordam and all it contains. Geartsje thinks the world is coming to an end. She holds on in the dark to one of the 161 upper berths; it's as if she's lifted way up with bed and all and then thrust down into a bottomless deep hole. The noise of her retching and that of many others is outdone by the moaning of the ship. Why in heaven's name are the men not allowed to join the women now? Why must all those young fathers remain in the hold as prisoners behind barred doors? Now and then it feels as if a plug shoots out of her ear, then she hears someone curse and yell loudly. Or is it only the provoked beast of the Noordam that curses? It courses through mountains and valleys of frothing wetness.

Among all the frightening noises, Frisian voices after all: "what's going to happen?" And: "I don't know, but we're in trouble."

When Geartsje has puked her insides out, she gets so caught up in confusion that she imagines having to vomit because she's pregnant with her twins Jacob and Hizkia. They seem still to be deep inside her, she hears again their shaky birth screams. She gropes the blankets covered with vomit, searching for both delicate bodies, for their little heads. She touches something. It's her three healthy children. Geartsje, she can't sit anymore, she can't lie down, retches again while there's nothing left to bring up. The last thing left of Geartsje Hiemstra-Namminga is her motherhood.

In the lower berth Grandma Ytsje suffers through the turmoil in fetal position. Groping, Geartsje goes in search of Mother's face. Her forehead feels cold, her eyes sunk back deep into their sockets appear lifeless, her mouth is sunken. On her chin here and there a spiny hair, and for the rest vomit. Alarmed, the daughter drops down on her knees before her mother's berth and begins to shake her bony shoulders. Behold, there's still life in the poor old soul. Not only that; after some throat clearing, Grandma raises her head and says: "We're in the middle of our punishment. The Lord our Lord chastises those whom he loves!"

Something seems wrong with the Noordam. It is rumored that in such a serious storm it can sail at only half its power, for otherwise it would bury itself so deep inside the enormous waves that it might never surface again.

"The ship is just trying to stay afloat."

Now and then a crewman comes with a portable lantern to do the same as a farmer does before turning in for the night: a visual check on his livestock. Only now do they discover the bad shape Grandma is in. Totally done in. For the first time the daughter has to wash and change the mother. Geartjse carefully pulls the smelly undervest over her head, and then there's still a flannel undershirt that needs changing.

Wait, what is that? Something drops out of a secret inside shirt pocket. A white envelope. A letter. From Springfield SD, delivered in Hichtum. The address written in ink is from none other than Lolke. Did Grandma in Hichtum hide a letter from Lolke? She must have. Why then didn't she open the envelope? Because there might have been an inconvenient truth inside? Geartsje takes hold of the envelope and pretends to know nothing.

Because of the extremely bad weather and other setbacks, the ocean journey takes a week longer than usual, but then the weather improves. After Grandma too has recovered, her first words are: "Are all of you still here?"

"Yes, we are, but we forgot the birthday of Nammen and Lys's little Anne; the child turned eight when the storm was at its worst."

"This passage is one giant baptism by immersion," Grandma observes, "the original sin has been washed away, and you can't think of a better birthday present."

And Geartsje all this time waiting for the question if a letter from America showed up when she was being cleaned. But Grandma is wiser than that; she thinks the less said the better.

With the ocean calming down, some men are beginning to feel carnally deprived. For fourteen days in a row the men were kept behind steel doors, without getting their way; most of them are not used to such a prolonged drought. Who managed a night ago to unlock that heavy steel door? And does an ocean steamer like this moan softly even in a gentle breeze?

What is that white shape that crawls underneath the blankets of upper berth 067 in the dead of night? And that while – how can it be helped – an old widow in lower berth number 066 has no intention to sleep? A fierce whisper from Grandma sends good advice to Douwe: "Douwe, that much commotion is not necessary!"

Later, at night, while Grandma snores her own dream, Geartjse and Douwe open the letter from Lolke in South Dakota, and read:

Dear family
[...] Here west of Springfield the summer seemed to run
its course so ideally, but now by us on Norwegian Hill the
bitter cold winter weather is getting the best of us. In the fall
we heard little good news from the Biesmas who live west of
Sioux Falls, and now nothing is heard from them at all any-
more. It's not likely that they crossed the Missouri, because
over there it's said to be even worse and twelve farm folk
were frozen to death. It is so bare and miserable here, every
sane person is heavyhearted. Think hard before you start,
tell our mother that. [...]

Dakota

On Wednesday morning, March 1, 1911, the Noordam glides past the Statue of Liberty into New York Harbor. It is clear, cool, and almost wind still. While Ellis Island – the island of tears – lies waiting a bit farther on, here and there a tear is already being wiped away. But in the huge customs warehouses everything runs like clockwork. After three hours all passengers, except for a few with medical, administrative, or personal issues, have set foot on American soil.

There they go, finally feeling the solid ground of the Land of Deliverance under their feet. How puny they feel against the surroundings of the huge skyscrapers; how insecure they are when they have to cross the wide avenue while cars come speeding from all directions.

Where are Nammen and Lys with the five kids?

"Look, they're still standing there, Nammen thinks he has to go in the opposite direction."

Douwe Hiemstra has his little firstborn Jacob on his arm, Grandma holds little Ytsje's hand, and Geartsje stands waiting with baby Hizkia on her arm: her three children, arriving in America with bare bottoms on account of the stolen diapers.

Geartsje watches how her mother, sure of herself – head held high like the old queen mother – starts walking. "We are where we're meant to be."

"Wait! You can't just cross like that, Grandma!"

"Trust in the Lord our Lord."

"But watch out in the meantime." Douwe is getting irritated. They stand waiting among a crowd of people.

"Where to?"

"Dakato!"

"Heck no, you're saying it wrong, it's Dakoate!"

"Take the train to Nebraska!"

"Heck no, we have to go to Dakoate."

They take a chance and cross the busy avenue. Two shabby men are eager to show them the way. While Douwe searches for his papers with the addresses, one of the men grabs the bag from Nammen's Lys. This time Nammen does not keep his cool; he's just a bit faster than the guy, delivers a blow and a kick, but comes back without the bag.

A couple of hours later both families are sitting dejected in an empty brick building behind the train station. There, under police guard, they have to spend their first American night.

"It is thus ordained for us," Grandma surmises, "we must first go through a kind of purgatory full of riffraff; tomorrow we arrive in the real America."

The real America. They're standing in Grand Central Station, ready to begin their train journey. To the city of Sioux Falls. It will be a matter of patience, the journey will last 33 hours. But then they're welcomed by a bright late winter sun; and there five adults stand with eight children in the middle of America on a nearly forsaken platform. Each one looks around cautiously, one even more worn out than the other. The shortage of diapers was supplemented in the train with pieces from Grandma's flannel undershirt and underpants. And still the old lady acts as if she knows nothing of the letter in the pocket of her undershirt.

While the whole group trudges to the exit, the last snowflakes float from a lone cloud in a nearly cleaned-up sky. Douwe and Nammen adjust their watches to the time on the Sioux Falls station clock. The clock strikes twelve. High noon. Grandma walks with the bow of her bonnet still straight under her chin. "We are now deep in America. Don't we have to unload our own moving crates here?"

"No," answers Nammen, "the railroad porters take care of that." He sticks a fresh wad behind his cheek, and with that he's out of tobacco.

Douwe is kind of quiet, worries about a good outcome, walks ahead of the group. "There are supposed to be two covered wagons waiting for us here with two pairs of horses." He shouts it out while he strides around the station. A bit later he meets the forlorn company again with an unsteady step. "Not a soul! No covered wagons, no horses, nothing! Are we at the right place?"

His question is silently processed, till suddenly the bewilderment oozes out on all sides. When the delegation somewhat clumsily enters the lonely station house through a couple of narrow folding doors, the doleful feeling overtakes them that they have indeed exited at the wrong station.

"Wait, damn it! Wait!" Nammen hollers as if he's yelling at a horse, but the train keeps going. "Our moving crates!" Too late, there go their belongings, the whole kit and caboodle.

"I believe we should've stayed on the train, but when it stopped here, Nammen thought he knew it all." Fortunately it is Nammen's Lys who says it. It takes a while before the confusion turns into dismay.

"I was thinking, those crates are not getting unloaded." Nammen kicks the double folding doors open, sees the train getting smaller and smaller, spits out his last wad of Jouster tobacco on the tracks, and again kicks open a self-closing door. Little Anna, the oldest of the group of kids, starts to scream like a mother who's lost her child; her play doll is still on the train.

"Shouldn't we have gotten out in Sioux City instead of Sioux Falls?" Geartsje asks herself aloud.

"I am sure that this is the right place," says Nammen, who not only has the papers in his pocket but also thinks he has them in his head.

"If the trip you have in your head is right, Nammen, then the train made a mistake!" Douwe has had it; the confusion almost causes a fight between them.

"Calm, children, we are in His hands, and we'll get to where we are supposed to be."

Douwe can't stand Mother-in-law anymore: "Right. I hear that we will be taken care of, so I'm going to have a nice nap," and he plants himself on a wooden bench in the station depot.

"Where is the toilet?" It's Grandma's attempt to calm everybody down. Douwe does his best not to say what he thinks, but he thinks: Go to the shithouse and put it in His hand.

"Does Douwe see that man walking over there?" Grandma asks when she returns from the toilet. "Douwe could try and find something out from that man." And Douwe goes ahead and does it too; it turns out that the man speaks the language of the Krauts, he studies Douwe's papers, and explains that in another four hours a train will leave from here to Yankton in South Dakota. That's the train they need to take. Their moving crates should be there for them and then they can travel in two large covered wagons to their final destination, Springfield, SD. It's as if the sun rises for the second time for the Hichtumers.

It's sixteen hours later, in the late night of March 5. Douwe and Nammen look at the station clock of Yankton and note that their watches are still in sync. An old lady with a basket stands in the wooden station building.

"The bread peddler of Yankton," Douwe concludes. The woman has fresh milk and a couple of loaves of bread that are still warm. Sure, she also has chewing tobacco. They have to do their eating and drinking on the go, for indeed, waiting for them in front of the station are two large covered wagons and a one-horse open flat wagon, with the moving crates already loaded.

"Namminga folk to Springfield, Hiemstra folk to Running Water," the driver cries with a shrill voice. He talks out of one side of his mouth, and chews with the other. Soon Douwe and Geartsje with the three children between them lie on a layer of straw in the bottom of a covered wagon. Plenty of blankets. Horse blankets. They're suddenly swallowed up in the night. They hear the wagon with Nammen and Lys take off. A whip slaps. "Go, go!"

"Running Water," cries the driver.

Douwe thinks they need to go to Springfield. "Running Water?"

"Yeah! Running Water!" The driver lowers the whip once more. "Go!"

"The kids are too tired to cry." Geartsje's words can hardly be heard above the racket. Douwe can still manage to stroke his courageous wife's cheek with a comforting touch. Is she shivering or crying? She weeps, she can no longer keep her emotions inside.

A couple of hours later they stop. And it's still pitch dark. Nammen and Lys's cargo transport stands in front of them. "Anybody needs to pee, now is the chance," someone shouts.

While behind him the three women squat on their heels, Douwe spies in the north a sliver of the waxing moon peeping out above an uneven horizon. A new day is knocking on the door. While each crawls back into their own nest, the barking of the prairie wolves can be clearly heard.

"Go, go!"

"We are in our Keeper's hand." Grandma Ytsje has moved from covered wagon 1 to covered wagon 2; now she lies across the bottom of Douwe and Geartsje's sleeping place. "We are going to share everything honestly," Lysbeth has just announced.

That morning at half past seven Douwe and Geartsje with their three children arrive at their address in the area of Running Water. Farther ahead, in a depression, the Missouri River lies glistening in the first light of morning. It's almost too much for Geartsje again. In what kind of town or region did Nammen and Lys with Grandma and the kids end up?

They themselves happened to have arrived on the Ulbe Eringa Farm. They can promptly pull up at the breakfast table. Eringa's prayer sounds like a sermon in a cathedral. Even after a detailed speech about church life, this farmer keeps talking. Sure, here, in this spot, he's seen bison in a herd of – now listen – thirty by fifty miles thunder across the prairie! He had seen them, but heard them coming too. "There they come! From the north, like an onrushing, irresistible flood wave of meat. Here in Running Water we thought first of a heavy storm approaching. It was just a rumbling to begin with, then it grew into an ear-deafening roar, and not much later it was like we were experiencing the end times. The uproar lasted a morning shift, so endless was the horde. Between Wolsey and Crow Lake there wasn't a house or tree still standing. I remember, first my wife's tea warmer stood shaking on the table, then the whole table began to shake. Oh oh, my wife's beautiful Makkum plate crashed from the wall, mind you – there lay her words of comfort in shards: 'Where'er on earth we run, o'er us shines the same sun.' We couldn't glue her words together again."

For the exhausted Hiemstras there's bread with lard, but no rest. And neither diapers. For Eringa was only responsible for the welcome, the sermon, and the stories. "Well, I'll bring you now to the Wijnia Farm, there's plenty work there for a farm laborer and his wife. All right! We'll see each other again in church tomorrow."

That same afternoon around mealtime they find themselves with the three little children on the Wijnia Farm. Again, Geartsje doesn't dare to mention sleep; and after all, for the first time in her life she's lodging somewhere. But Douwe takes the chance. "It's high time that my wife and kids get a little sleep in their system."

But no, the dinner table is ready. "The river!" Wijnia begins. "We can't quite see the Missouri River from here, but sometimes we can sure hear it. Watch out, I'm warning you now!" This farmer can team up with his neighbor Eringa, he imitates the sound of a galloping herd of bison. "On the other side of the Missouri is Nebraska. It's better here than in Nebraska."

Mrs. Wijnia has rice porridge, or something that looks like it. Each may fill up their plate from the same cast iron pot. Wijnia plants himself at the end of the long dining table and closest to the pot. There is his own holy seat. To silence his large household the man merely needs to clear his throat. As one very much in charge, he looks around, and commands: "Respect for God!", folds his hands,

70

and in a wide-ranging prayer makes mention of a blessed trip from Hichtum to Springfield. Amen.

In the same tone of voice he continues to give a local weather report. "Nature here is a force, not a month ago we nearly died from the cold, the sow with eleven piglets froze to death in the barn, and I mean hard frozen baby pigs, the prairie wolves would've broken their teeth on them. And here in the summer we have the tornadoes…"

Mrs. Wijnia adds: "With the last cyclone neighbor Jouko Svendrup's little girl died."

But then Wijnia comes back with: "Yeah! Wat de Lord us gives to kerrie kin we chust take!"

Again, hands folded and respect, now for giving thanks. During the prayer Douwe dares to open his eyes and glance at the forsaken prairie through the small window. The way the land looks here must be the way it first saw light after the Flood. He feels himself drenched in a wave of emotion, and he thinks to himself: we shouldn't have done this.

An hour and a half later Douwe Hiemstra, formerly milker in Hichtum, is farm laborer and Geartjse a maid for day and night on the Wijnia Farm in Running Water. It lasts for a week, then it turns out that the ex-milker has already appropriated something of the harshness of this place: "Wijnia, I can make a lot more on the Lee Nickel Farm, so I'm going to leave with wife and kids."

"Then off with you!" Wijnia is getting angry; his other half stays milder: "Oh, how ungrateful!" She says it while she snatches the plates off the table. What Douwe says next is nothing like Geartsje has ever heard him say before; he quotes Meindert Birdie: "It's been drummed into me here: Whoever makes himself into a sheep is going to be eaten by wolves!"

When the Nickel boys pick them up the same day with horse and wagon, they stand ready, fully packed. Douwe's goodbye words: "If we should meet each other again, it will be in church."

Half a year later Douwe and Geartsje move to the Tommy Jones Farm for ten dollars more a month, and after that it's on to the large town of Avon, for there they can lay their hands on eighty acres of good farmland for a moderate price. First renting it, of course. As one who came from Penjum, Douwe seeds it first with wheat, but by harvest time the price of grain has gone south. After a couple of months Geartsje's household ledger is in bad shape. Poverty. If the oldest children hadn't come home twice a week from the Thys Bakker Farm with a gallon of soup, they would have been at hunger's door.

On a Sunday morning after church, Douwe bumps into a side job: he can become gravedigger in the cemetery of the fast-growing village of Avon. Digging graves with his self-forged terp spade after a Hichtum design. At the time he does not know that the first casualties of a worldwide epidemic will be coming his way.

"It could be a plague or something," he says one evening. "I have four graves to dig tomorrow." Millions of people around the world will succumb to the aggressive Spanish flu, and the states of South Dakota and Nebraska are not spared. Thus it's death that helps them to survive. During this time two more healthy children join the family, making it a total of five.

When Douwe comes home later than usual one night in 1916, Geartsje notices that he's not well. He lacks appetite and has trouble sleeping. It's as if she sees her own dad in him, father Hizkia who from all the setbacks could also hit rock bottom. What if Douwe himself should have caught the deadly flu? It didn't take long for the truth to surface: "Geartsje, I can't take this job anymore, the grief in the cemetery kills me." In just a week he's had to dig who knows how many children's graves.

And so Douwe leaves the dead of Avon and moves his young family to Norwegian Hill. There, in the middle of nowhere, an abandoned farm is for sale. They take it; they don't ask why it has been abandoned.

In the summer of 1917 on Norwegian Hill Douwe has recovered his old self again. At the bottom of the hill there's a hundred acres of good farmland for sale, nicely located in the low part next to the Missouri. The price is negotiable, and he's in luck. "Good luck with the purchase," says the owner. "Blessings with the money," says the buyer. Here, on this good piece of land they can have some cows too. In October Douwe takes a chance and sows eighty acres with winter wheat, for the first time seeding his own land. A winter follows with the temperature at times dipping to forty below, but the wheat turns out to be so hardy that the crop comes up nice and even.

It's a warm Sunday afternoon in the last part of July 1918, when a hot prairie wind blows around Norwegian Hill; in the hollow the Missouri shimmers in the backlight. The Rocky Mountains are apparently generous with water again – the river is lively as a deer. Together the farmer and his wife stroll to the top of the hill and see, deep in the hollow, their wheat field, undulating in the hot wind. Their golden triangle, the fruit of their toil in sweat and tears. The crop is ripening, almost three feet high. Together they walk down the slope toward their wheat field.

In the distance against the slope, the dark red of their house with barn and cowshed contrasts against a steel-blue sky. "Grandma is taking care of the kids," she says, "I think that she can see us."

"What a wonderful promising crop," he says.

"Nobody can surprise us here," she says. "Come." He understands. They do it, in their own ripening grain.

While they're still enjoying the afterglow, he says: "If anybody outside the Creator has seen us, it's Grandma. It takes a rascal to know a rascal."

"No, Grandma is taking the kids along to Hichtum this afternoon, she's telling them her old stories!"

"Grandma would say: 'We hold the winning cards with what we have accomplished.'"

That evening after mealtime, when outside it's still as soft as silk, the farmer and his wife trot back up to the top of the hill and watch how in the west the Missouri disappears as a silver thread on the horizon. They stand there till the sun has descended so far that the silver thread changes to gold. "It's growing fast and the weather is steady," he says, "we can harvest it by the end of this week."

When Geartsje that evening is about to close the bedroom curtains, she sees that, like a gigantic ball, the sun lets itself be swallowed by the earth. The golden thread turns red. Blood red. When she begins to talk to Douwe about it and looks around, Douwe is already asleep. On top of the blankets, in his long white underwear. She pulls the bedroom curtain shut and thinks she glimpses lightning. "We might get a shower," she says to herself, "that's just what we need, Douwe."

A good two days later, during the night of Tuesday to Wednesday, the barking of their Scottish collie Birdie wakes them up. The barking becomes a howling cry. Douwe shoots out of bed and strides barefoot across the yard. He hears noise behind the wooden barn. He goes down, and the murmur turns into a roar. The Missouri! Now he dashes down the hill with huge strides.

When some fifteen minutes later he resurfaces in his underwear, Geartsje has come to meet him. "The Missouri," he pants, "the Missouri has ripped all of our land with it. Geartsje, my dear, we've lost everything." All their hopes and expectations have been torn away, every scrap of land, by a roaring river. The mighty 2,300-mile-long Missouri was simply following its normal course. It went awry where the Niobrara, the tributary, joins the main river. And just at the place lay their golden triangle.

But just as a healthy tree always grows new leaves, so Douwe and Geartsje will gather new courage; that same year they return to the forsaken Tommy Jones Farm to try again, through hard work and smart farming. Geartsje earns extra money by peddling cream and eggs in a milk cart in Avon. If Douwe ever brags, he brags about his Geartsje. "Whether we have the wind behind us or against us, Geartsje means everything to me."

Early November 1919. They were able to rent some additional land. And then winter hits. Forty degrees below on top of a knee-high layer of snow. In the meantime Douwe has more than one in Geartsje: any day now another child may come and this time she is so heavy, she hardly knows what to do.

And in this kind of winter weather, will midwife, nurse, and counselor Grandma Ytsje, who's staying with Lolke, be able to make it in time? Well, all right, Grandma's children are always glad to see the old lady come – and also glad to see her go again, so Lolke takes a chance with the old lady next to him in the buggy. "Go, go!" This time he can make it across the frozen creek, which saves him fifteen minutes of travel time.

"Gosh, Douwe," he exclaims when he sees Geartsje's swollen belly, "you didn't do half a job there."

Midwife Grandma lays her wooden stethoscope on Geartsje's bare belly, listens intently, and makes her diagnosis. "Geartsje, I hear your sixth child say to your seventh that they're going to come together. It sounds like two big boys."

"Dr. Greendale from Avon is certain that it's not twins."

"It's twins. I'll tell you this: if this is one baby, then it's going to be murder." Grandma never doubts. "I have never seen an expectant mother so awfully big, so I would say: Daughter, hold fast to the proverb from the time of King Hezekiah: Whoever trusts in the Lord will receive protection."

Fourteen days later Geartsje has become only heavier. And again a snowstorm blows in. "A change in the weather, that will make it come," Grandma predicts. But the weather turns so bad that all the farms southeast of Avon are cut off from the rest of the world. The two oldest of the five children, Jacob and Ytsje, can just make it to neighbor Claus Brandt after school, and that's where they stay.

What if it turns out badly with Geartsje and Doctor Greendale can't come… the thought makes Douwe and Geartsje sick to their stomach; the drama with the two boys in Hichtum preys on their mind again. In the meantime Geartsje becomes so uncomfortable, she can hardly stay on her feet. Only for the sake of sharing their worries, Douwe harnesses the horse in front of the buggy and takes a chance on the trip to the Claus Brandt Farm.

Brandt plays the optimist but is deeply worried; he heard from neighbor Olle Kolson that the redskins expect a third blizzard. "I've made up my mind," he says with feigned cheer, "I'm going to harness my horse and ride with my buggy behind you, and then we'll see if we can get Geartsje to old Doctor Greendale in Avon before nighttime. Let her give birth there, she'll be in good hands."

Both of the men haven't been underway for more than fifteen minutes when the snow starts falling. The wind picks up so much that there's no way to get through anymore. Claus Brandt has to turn back and Douwe has to pull out all the stops to make it back safely to his farm.

"It's coming!" says Grandma while he follows her to the delivery bed.

"Outside there's no way to get anywhere anymore," he says. Suddenly the old lady stops, turns around and points up: "In all your travels acknowledge Him, and He shall direct your paths!"

The night is bitter cold, the howling of the snow storm mixes with the desperate cries of the woman trying to give birth. Wait a minute, is that a thunder clap? Now what! Something heavy clatters down in the upstairs loft. As if it were a wheelbarrow full of bricks, it couldn't be worse. Douwe rushes to the kitchen and discovers that the chimney has collapsed. The flue plugs up, the house fills with smoke, he can't see his hand in front of his eyes anymore. Besides all this, it sounds as if someone is kicking against the outside door. Douwe hardly knows what to do anymore. He rushes to the door, sees two seriously frozen scarecrows standing on the stoop. From their voices he can hear that they are Claus Brandt and Olle Kolson. "It took us five hours, but we have the old doctor here!" At the same moment Dr. Greendale stumbles through a smoke curtain into the debris-strewn kitchen. "We got him here, but don't ask how." Claus Brandt can't help but feel proud.

"First of all, get the stove out of here!" the frozen doctor croaks.

"This is going to be a tough birth," Claus Brandt predicts.

Indeed, it takes nearly an hour for the men to get the stove outside in the snow. And a good hour later Grandma emerges from the side room with birth news: "A great big boy! I'd say at least ten pounds, and I'm talking Frisian pounds. I think it should be a Nammen."

When the old lady disappears again in the wings, the smoke has dissolved enough for Olle Kolson and Claus Brandt to make a grab for the old whisky bottle. "Come on, Douwe, the women will take care of it!"

"Cheers!"

A half hour later Grandma is back: "Another big boy! Another heavy one. This should be a Lolke, Douwe!" Doctor estimates the boys together at nearly eighteen pounds. And Geartsje is doing great. "Only, the old doctor is exhausted, so I tucked him in next to Geartsje in Douwe's place."

"Douwe, come on, for us a good-sized double too."

"Cheers!"

"As long as I have you here now," begins Grandma Ytsje Namminga-Wytsma, "I want to give you some good advice: If you as man and wife want to yield to each other's desire, you should do it after the day's work in the evening. Not in the daytime, and never outside, that only makes for hefty babies.

SMOLDERING RUINS

End of February 1919. Johannes Boorsma is a Frisian among the Frisians again. As long as it lasts. On the way to his small houseboat on the Franeker Canal below Ysbrechtum he hears the call of the first oyster catcher. What a mild late winter! And there is also less pleasant news: he will have to tell his wife pretty soon that he just lost his farm job and is now unemployed.

As laborer with Freark Boschma on Him Road below IJlst he had finished his work that evening around six, but when he was getting ready to go home, the farmer's wife asked him if he would take the time to butcher the calf.

Johannes never takes long to decide, so he said: "OK, I'll still do that." An hour and a half later he reported through the backdoor that he'd got the job finished. All the calf meat and what goes with it he had put neatly in three clean buckets inside the door. There came the farmer's wife: "The boss says that it's high time for you to go home now."

"Is that all, Missus?"

Mrs. Boschma had already turned away but apparently the farmer stood right behind her, and she called back: "The boss says, all right then, let Johannes take the calf head along to the houseboat."

But Johannes blurted out: "Let the boss and his wife get their fill on calf's brains themselves, both could use a little more brains!"

He's already gathering his milking clothes and other belongings together, stuffs them in his empty flour sack, and makes his way through the wet fields to his little houseboat named 'Meadow and Water.'

When he delivers the bad news to his Pytsje pretty soon, she will say: "Johannes, my boy, did it have to go this way?"

"Yes," he will reply, "in this case it had to."

As he thinks about it, a twinge of pity shoots through his breast:

not self-pity, but pity for her. Pytsje, with her yearning for peace. She's the only one who can calm the lion, but she's not nearly always successful. And still she's behind him all the way and gives him all her support.

It's a dark, moonless night; the path to the houseboat leads over uneven polder dikes, along muddy tracks, and across wide water-filled ditches. Oh no, he feels the sludge seep into his clogs, but this time his dreams are not to be undone by a couple of wet feet.

In his dream the image of a magical landscape beneath steel-blue summer skies rises before his eyes. Against a backdrop of high snow-topped mountains stands a barn, a cow shed with a covered haymow beside it. A horse is harnessed to a showy carriage, a flag with stars and stripes is waving in the wind, a couple of children playing between cattle and flowers, swallows high in the air like phantoms against the deep blue. Does he hear the call of the golden plover now? You bet, gliding from the mountains comes a huge congregation of golden plovers. They've arrived home after a journey over sea and land. And among them, a solitary 'comfort bird.'

He sees his dad and mom standing in the yard, Meindert Birdie and Willemke van Zandbergen. Proudly she points to the mountains. Sure enough, there against the high slopes lies the forsaken village. Hichtum has joined the emigration, the church with its gabled roof, the summer-green beech hedge circling the cemetery, just a bit higher than the highest tombstone. And strewn around the terp and canal, a handful of homes. "It's possible after all!" He hears his dad exclaim. "I was able to take my soul with me."

Johannes feels the Ysbrechtum mire run into his clogs again. What kind of foolish dream was this? Did this dream awaken a secretly hidden longing in him? America? He keeps going, confused now. His dad was not good enough for America according to the mayor; the old man's longing turned into resentment, if it wasn't hate. No America for Dad, then not for me either. Don't talk to me about America. Then rather Germany!

There, in the Ruhr District, he lived like a libertine. Wandering from job to job and not a Mark to his name. Same with the women: from one onto the other. He wanted to become a German among the Germans, but as a newspaper reader he also went from one to the other: from the *Kevelaerer Blatt* he switched to the *Rheinische Post*, then *Die Glocke*, and the last year to the *Kölnische Rundschau*. In search of the true one and the truth. He was getting closer to feeling what animated the Germans, but for some reason or other it would not become like home. After he saw the cannon fodder march in columns to the trenches of the First World War in 1914, he was back in his home yard. The way his dad in his coffin was entrusted to the Hichtum soil under the song of the golden plover, that's how he also loved this damn land.

Not a playboy after all.

He came home with a mustache like that of the German Kaiser. A summons to military service lay on Mom's plush tablecloth. In the neutral Netherlands he had to be mobilized. Not good enough for calf's meat, but good enough for cannon fodder. When the selection officer asked him what kind of work he had done, he smelled his chance and answered: "Skipper." Marine life attracted him. As the successor to gardener Piter Kamstra from Burchwert he had after all punted the shit pram for fourteen days from Burchwert, Hichtum, and Hartwert to the sewage dump at Himertille. He had done it to help Piter out of a pickle, not for the mayor's shit.

How free is the soldier's life? First he landed in Sneek, then Enkhuizen, after that Terschelling, and finally Laaksum, "that lovely Place that would bring me so much Happiness." That's how it was described in his diary.

In late summer 1915 he saw Pytsje Jongsma come biking up the Warnzer Cliff. "Where are you headed?" He called after her. She could've just kept biking, was cheeky enough, had worked in Amsterdam as a house maid, but she stopped. A handsome young man in uniform laid his hand close to hers on the handlebars. With his stern, perfectly trimmed mustache he looked more like a general than a soldier. And she, she was a tall young lady with eyes the color of the South Sea beneath a northwind-swept spring sky.

After that they became inseparable. In mid-September 1916 they biked together to Koudum to give their marriage notice, and that was high time, for on April 6, 1917, a beautiful daughter was born to them. Lysbeth. On April 24 followed his honorable discharge from 'service with the militia.' Not enough money for a house, but enough for a little old sailboat. Pytsje always gave him space, but that evening she said: "For our child's sake both of us must be responsible and aim for stability."

So a steady job with a farmer. And then it started again: from one farmer to the next. Always and everywhere the pitcher would be filled with water till it broke: "Let the boss and his wife get their fill on calf's brains themselves."

And now he has to deliver black tidings to Pytsje again. Fired, while she's about to give birth. Not a penny of income anymore. In the darkness he can already see the contours of the houseboat rise above the flat land. It appears that out of sheer thrift she hasn't yet lit the kerosene lamp. Wait a minute, the baby's birth must not take place today or tomorrow in this drafty houseboat on the Franeker Canal. And it's even anchored by Freark Boschma's field. From one moment to the next he feels the break with the farmer as a liberation. Their little boat lies in an open waterway, the streams are free of ice again, there's no place that ties them down, no home that has a hold on them, no person he needs to bow to. All he has to do is to untie the boat and be off.

Without the reward of even an ounce of veal for Pytsje, he stands before the gang plank, and suddenly he remembers that he dug up five fat moles during his lunch break. He gets down on one knee on the gang plank, digs out his pocket knife and helps the creatures out of their coats. With the skins he steps onboard, shoves the hatch aside and calls: "Good news, five nice moleskins and a good mood." After he lets himself down into the hold, he turns the flame of the lamp higher.

81

"You're late! The baby is here already."

He takes the kerosene lamp from the hook, turns the flame higher and lights up the scene.

"Good God, Pytsje." There she lies, on a mattress on the floor, with a cloth-wrapped baby, the umbilical cord still tied to the mother.

"It's a healthy child," she reports calmly.

He flings the moleskins onto the counter, grabs a handful of green soap from the soap dish, darts through the hatch outside, washes his hands in the Franeker Canal, and afterward does what his wife calmly and quietly tells him to do. She appears to have everything prepared: scissors, bellyband, clean bedding, cloths, diapers. She even has warm water that's already boiled on the stove.

"I have to get in the scow to fetch the midwife from Turns."

"Not necessary," she says calmly, "tomorrow I'll be back on my feet."

"And otherwise I'll be here, I read the riot act to the farmer and his wife."

"I had expected as much."

Though he badly wants to know whether it is a boy or a girl, he doesn't ask her about it, and makes no further effort to find out. He dropped hints in the past that he badly hoped for a son.

"It's a healthy baby," she repeats. And isn't that more than enough?

An hour and a half later mother and child are resting, clean and peaceful. Before bedtime, he has a duty to fulfill. He gets into the scow and crosses the Franeker Canal. After all, the afterbirth is too precious to him to bury it in Freark Boschma's field.

When he's back in the floating birth room, she says: "Are you aware that we got ourselves a little fowler?" And she names his name.

He nearly loses his voice when the boy's name is announced: "Meindert, Meindert Birdie."

He has the Boorsma habit of checking out the weather before turning in for the night. This time he does so only to breathe in his deep happiness all alone. With his back turned to the cold north, he's staring in southwesterly direction, and a feeling descends on him that there, in that black emptiness, lies their future anchoring place. Back in the old polder – the Heidenskip, nearly at the end of the world, on the bank of the Aant Liuwe Pool, at small farmer and dreamer Freark Smink's mill yard. Isn't it possible that a room with two beds may become available before Alde Maaie*? Freark had told him casually, but only now does he value the importance. Maybe he could get used to living in the mill with Pytsje and both kids. Better sell the 'Meadow and Water' then, it's about ready to sink any day anyway. As a miller he would have only one boss, and that's the wind. However rough and changeable that gentleman could be, Johannes 'Kaiser' would adjust himself to it. Milling some 500 acres of land, picking up some odd jobs, catching some moles and polecats and golden plovers – the future smiles at him again.

"All is settled," he says in German, when with a feeling of full contentment he takes one more look at his wife and children that night.

It's almost midnight when Johannes Boorsma thinks of one more thing. He raises his bike from the hold, pushes it through the marshy ground to the roadway, and pedals to Hichtum to tell his old mother Willemke that there's a Meindert again.

"There comes Her Majesty's 'Meadow and Water,' with the Kaiser himself at the helm." Freark Smink, who runs a small farm in the Heidenskip Commons, isn't the kind of farmer who just stares out of the window to count sheep. And should he count the sheep, he quickly loses count. Freark is both farmer and poet at the same

---

* May 1 was traditionally the day in Friesland that land leases and employment contracts started and ended. It was moving day throughout the province. When in 1700 the old Julian calendar was replaced by the Gregorian one, the year shifted by twelve days. To prevent contracts from being cut short by twelve days, the big moving day shifted with the calendar. Henceforth May 12 would be the big moving day, known as *Alde Maaie* (Old May) in contrast with *Nije Maaie* (New May), the new May 1.

time. Sometimes he stands by the window and gets lost in dreams, imagining a performance of a play on one of the islands in the Fluezen.

Still that same evening, this Freark with his wife Grytsje van der Weg trots to the Aant Liuwe Pool where the 'Meadow and Water' has found a resting place. Pytsje served as a farm maid with the Sminks in the last year before her wedding, after she had learned to eat with knife and fork as maidservant to mayor Antonie Roëll in Amsterdam. With Freark and Gryt she unlearned those manners again. And then one evening she came with Johannes, the soldier. One time when Freark was in need of a milker, the soldier came on Her Majesty the Queen's time to milk the eight cows. The farmer and the Kaiser really hit it off together.

And now he's come as commander of the 'Meadow and Water.' Freark judges that the bottom of the little sailboat is close to letting water seep through.

"We float, and that's about it." Johannes laughs it off.

"Watch out, there's nothing worse than a leaky boat and an angry wife."

Freark's Gryt lets herself down into the 'Meadow and Water' with two pints of milk, a loaf of bread, and her knitting. "Now what do we have here, a new crew member!" The talk about the childbirth gets right to the point, just like the delivery itself. And then the men, too, lower themselves and exclaim that the junior seaman needs to be toasted. It turns out that here, way in the back polder, there's still 16 oz. of gin around; the women will have to make do with goat milk.

There's no standing room in the frigate, Freark decides. A small table with four tiny chairs with legs that have been shortened by six inches, a bed, two cribs against the wall for the kids, a kerosene lamp swinging in languid motion to the waves of the Aant Liuwe Pool.

"The mill, a place to live, and the milling," Johannes begins. "Come on, Freark, now we're still sober."

84

Freark: "The mill and the living arrangements are free. As far as that goes, you can move in there tonight if you want. And what's expected from you? Milling! For the rest it's up to you. Otherwise, why don't you sail this barge first to the Wildschut dock on Gaast Lake, Johannes. Last time you said yourself that the thing is beginning to get as leaky as an old woman."

Johannes considers: "Free lodging at the mill, a gallon of milk per week on top of that. At the expense of the polder commission, you won't get stuck with that, Freark. On these conditions I'll see to it that here on the commons children will never come home again with wet feet."

"Cheers!"

"Zum Wohl!" Johannes knows that here in the Heidenskip there are always odd jobs available.

In Workum and surroundings people find it strange that a farmer like Freark Smink gets along so well with that blustery day laborer. A boorish fellow like Johannes Kaiser should be taught his place, but no, he addresses the farmer as an equal as if it were the most natural thing in the world. And that while in the Frisian Southwest corner the farmer's wife, till the day she dies, addresses her own husband as 'sir'.

Johannes and Freark waste little time talking about the weather, and turn to politics. Freark confides in his friend that he switched from the Reformed Church party to the secular democrats, the movement that leans toward national disarmament. And now the farmer would like to know what Johannes thinks of 'Germany today,' where after WWI "the ruins are still smoldering."

"My dear Freark, a time will come when the Germans will lash out again. I know, you're leaning toward the broken gun, but not I! After the signing of the Versailles peace treaty in 1919 I don't believe in peace anymore. With that treaty the Germans are even more humiliated; as losers they're being undressed by the French and now as well by a growing power like America. That's going to turn into war again. I'm telling you: humankind and war are inextricably connected."

"But Johannes, do you know how many young people fell in action within a couple of weeks just at Verdun? More than 200,000! Every one of them a fine young man! Such a thing should never, never happen again. Get rid of the guns!"

"If you want peace, you've got to be willing to have war."

Pytsje: "Talk about something else!"

Grytsje: "Yes, why don't you talk about music instead?"

Two men who differ widely, but who hang on to each other. Freark sees Johannes as a man of the world, the man who at the cathedral in Cologne saw the soldiers return from the front. He saw them go with roses in the barrels of their guns. Johannes was there; the Frisian boy who before his 25th birthday had made love to German young ladies and farmer widows of all sorts and sizes, according to the stories he'd heard him tell. And that same boy can read German papers, even whole books.

"All right, music it is," sighs Freark. "Johannes, you've heard the great orchestras over there."

"Music, you better believe it."

"Johannes, a while ago I heard some serious music too, by one of the greatest composers in Germany and Austria. Beethoven! It came through the gramophone of Mr. Gaastra from the tea company in Workum. 'His Master's Voice,' was the name of the music."

"That's the name of Gaastra's gramophone," Grytsje contributes. "Freark was invited to come to Gaastra to listen and had to cry, he found the music that beautiful."

"I like to listen to the violin," Johannes admits. "But it shouldn't be too highfalutin. Actually, the most beautiful music can come from one bird."

The twenties. Never before has Johannes Kaiser lived so long at one and the same address as at the mill with Freark Smink. The milk route for the Workum Cooperative, 'Good Expectation' flourishes and delivers a basic income. Day in and day out the milk cans of eighteen farms hustle through the hands of the Kaiser.

In his diary he puts it this way:

> *We're having a rich Time here in the Polder. Pietje and I are enjoying a nice Household, and the Children love the School in Brandeburen, even though the Farm Children are sometimes favored.*

All goes well, until the milk factory board outsources the milk route anew.

"Now what?"

He's out. Is Johannes not good enough anymore? 'His' farmers sign the manifest 'Johannes must stay.' But one person doesn't sign it, and that one is on the factory board. Johannes has had a dispute with him. Because the farmer often overslept in the morning, the milk hauler regularly got to the factory too late. And that's why he often came home late, when the kids were already in bed. At first the deputized milk hauler broached the problem with a quip, but on a Thursday morning Johannes had had his fill and came to this final conclusion: "There are two kinds of failed farmers: the one gets up but is still asleep, the other wakes up but doesn't get up." And that cooked his goose.

Johannes is sure that Freark will now have his milk delivered to one of the private milk factories in the area. But for Freark the Cooperative was an important part of his philosophy of life.

"What are you waiting for, Freark!"

"Johannes, my man, I live as a sharecropper on the Van der Feltz farmstead, and my landlord is very sympathetic to the Workum Cooperative. If because of this incident I switch to a private butter factory, Van der Feltz will knock me from his farm on May 12."

"Are you afraid to point out to that aristocrat that a milk hauler here who for years never overslept is being kicked to the side? If your landlord is truly a nobleman he will straighten out that company board."

"And that he won't do. I can't afford to get into trouble with the landlord, he can make and break me." Deadly pale and without saying another word Johannes disappears into his house by the mill.

Freark too is out of sorts, he can't sleep a wink. When early the next morning he stares out of the window, he is shocked to see that Johannes has set the mill in its mourning position. In a panic he hurries into his wooden shoes, strides nervously to the mill yard, and discovers that the house is empty. The Kaiser has vanished. His fishing boat is also gone. Freark and Gryt feel sick. The next day all of the Heidenskip community knows about the silent exodus: "They appear to live now in that little boat that for ages has lain in neglect by the Nijhuzum Bridge."

It is 1929 now. Johannes and Pytsje live in a larger and newer houseboat with their six children. Its name 'Meadow and Water' has expanded to BICYCLE SALES AND REPAIR SHOP J. BOORSMA. In the evening the Hepkema paper is tossed through the boat's door, once a week supplemented with the Sunday edition of the *Rheinische Post*.

A couple of years later. In Germany the ruins continue to smolder and the wounds continue to smart. That's how it's put in the Rheinische Post, but according to the Kaiser it won't be long before the roses will bloom again. "Remember man, all I have to say is shit, and I'm Heimatberechtigt, have German right of residence".

"What are you talking about, Kaiser!"

"Let me tell you exactly what I mean. In the end, you and I will need the National Socialists in Germany. When they get into power, then the farmer and his hired man will both ride in the same kind of beautiful car." The farmer who's listening to this will pedal past the Kaiser's Repair Shop, even if he has two flat tires, for the farmer in no way wants to ride in the same car as his hired man. And that's how Johannes Meinderts Boorsma, on the way to his ideal, relegated his own fate to the dustbin.

On a humid Saturday evening in the late summer of 1929, Dad and Mom and all six children sit at the dining table in their houseboat. The oldest, Lysbeth at twelve, faces the prospect of leaving home to go to work as a farm maid in the near future. Dad has already found a place for her with the Bajemas in Ferwâlde. The youngest, a girl who at Dad's insistence is named after her mom, is not yet two years old.

"Dad, a man's getting off his bike and is coming to the door." Son Meindert, now ten, overhears what the man is coming for. "I'm interested in a new bike." The customer is a young man of about eighteen. "I want the Union brand bike that you've been displaying for some weeks."

"That's good," Johannes says cheerfully. He hauls the bike outside. "I don't know you," says Johannes, "are you from Workum?"

"Originally from Koudum. But don't worry, Boorsma, I'll pay you right away, I would like to take it with me tonight. I can handle it with one hand on each handlebar. It's a hundred and fifteen guilders, right?"

"That's right. OK, let me pump up the tires for you."

The young man takes the money out of his inside pocket, counts the amount out on the workbench, makes a few comments about the humid weather, and is ready to take off with the new bike.

"Is the bike for yourself?" Johannes wants to know.

"No, for my boss; I work for Freark Smink in the Heidenskip."

"Wait a minute," Johannes calls out, "that changes things."

A good fifteen minutes later the young man finally takes off with the new bike, but now outfitted with double cycle bags and – for the coming winter – a couple of new hand warmers with wool lining inside to boot. "And don't forget to give greetings to the farmer and his wife from Johannes and Pytsje."

"So," Pytsje sighs afterward. "The discord with the Sminks has plagued us long enough."

The Dust Bowl

The twenties, but then on the other side of the ocean. America is trying with all its might to become a world power, and it looks like all Americans want to get in on the act. Douwe – as the American David – risks putting himself behind the wheel of his third-hand Model A Ford, and Geartsje sits behind her Singer American pedal sewing machine – two ingenious machines that nearly make the same humming sound. It is the song that celebrates American optimism and progress. Grandma Ytsje, who sticks to psalms and hymns, tries with warnings and admonitions to keep her flock on the narrow path. "Douwe in a luxury car! Oh vanity of vanities, it is all vanity."

David Hiemstra, now farming on the Tommy Jones Farm which has been hastily re-baptized the David Hiemstra Farm, ventures out on his maiden trip and races into the yard in his Model A. He has to stop but can't find the brake; he hollers "stop" with all his might, but the vehicle does not listen. And so David crashes right through a wooden rigging into the barn. Four chickens dead, and the Ford is now fourth-hand. The 'Memories' of the Hiemstras will record that Dad David bit his bent pipe in half.

We're in the Roaring Twenties, but the farm people with a view of the Missouri hardly notice. The Charleston makes the dance halls in Sioux Falls and Rapid City shake, but for the pioneering farm folk there is no time for that kind of nonsense. And the local paper may well assert that the female corset is out of fashion, but Geartsje has never had one of those around her body. And Douwe is not at all sorry about that; nothing beats nature.

Is it possibly different in Hichtum and the Himert neighborhood? Are they aware that the same Charleston is being danced in Sipke Castelein's establishment on South Square in Leeuwarden? It's true, for globalization is on the way. It's in the air. Even if the ocean is still a frightening immensity.

A change occurs on a Friday morning. Let's call it a shock. May 27, 1927. Old Olle Kolson, normally as calm as cod-liver oil, comes stumbling into the Hiemstra yard with the astonishing news: "The radio! The radio reported that Charles Lindbergh made it across the ocean in his airplane!" The Swedish immigrant is emotional. "Lindbergh is a hero!" He who's not afraid of challenges in the New World will make his way. That's the mindset of the immigrant – catalyst of American optimism. "Go, go!"

Hizkia and Ytsje's Geartsje from Hichtum knows that she will never cross the ocean again. Once, but never again. Not on a steamboat, not in a Zeppelin, and especially not in an airplane. Only her thoughts at times still cross the ocean: in her field of vision rises a stubby tower and other images of the past in all their colorful detail, she hears forgotten voices, and then she's attacked by a sickness that defies easy description. It chafes somewhere in the place where her soul must be located. It can happen to her just like that, like a cloud that's about to slide in front of the sun, when the mailman hands her a letter, for example, from widow Willemke Boorsma van Zandbergen from Hichtum. In the envelope that smells like the whole of Friesland there are a few words in the old language and an old picture postcard with the stubby tower on it and across from the cemetery gate a woman by the door. Abe Annes, that must be her. A frozen past melts. This time it is a message from Willemke.

[...] When the sounds of the colorful thrush woke me up this morning, I thought, would Meindert be hearing this now too. [...] Do you have thrushes there too? It's a terribly dry summer here, Jan Mensonides says there are such deep cracks in the ground, you can hear the dogs bark in America, but Geertje, it can't be that bad, right [...] Well Geertje, with two lively boys added to your household at the same time you must be thinking sometimes that's about enough.

Well, I hear the Hichtum tower toll twelve o'clock, but I bet
you still remember, Hichtum in the summertime is about
ten minutes fast, the farmers prefer it that way. [...]

The courage and the persistence of Douwe and Geartsje Hiemstra
were rewarded: in the twenties they enjoy a favorable spring three
years in a row. Farm production in the Midwest is doubled, the
production of the David Hiemstra Farm as well. The older ones of
the eight children all pitch in. In the meantime almost every village
now has a bank branch.

"Well Geartsje, I'm inclined to make an investment too."

"Go ahead!" And there goes Douwe, behind the wheel of Henry
Ford's miracle, on the way to Avon to make an investment. In the
backseat are twins Nammen and Lolke, born in the snowstorm at
the end of November 1919. They're from two eggs but speak one
language: Frisian. They don't just speak their mother tongue, but
especially their grandmother tongue as well. The twins are already
farming their own little place, even if it's just for fun: their Frisian
pedigree cattle is made from black and white painted pieces of cow
bone.

Old Doctor Greendale from Avon came up with a nickname for
the small gentleman farmers: 'The Blizzard Boys.' The doctor feels
attached to these twins; a picture of both boys hangs in his office.
One need only glance at it and the doctor comes out with the story
that the boys were born during the by now legendary snow storm
of 1919 in a temperature of 40 below and that together they weighed
nearly twenty pounds. And that mother Gertrude Hiemstra can be
named 'world champion new mother': Gave birth today to two big
babies – one of ten pounds and the other over eight – and tomorrow back to milking cows. And then that singular Granny. She had
tucked him in that late night right next to the new mother, and he
had slept like a log.

"But there's a condition attached," the doctor must have added.

If all those sturdy kids on the David Hiemstra Farm want to become American, they're going to have to learn better English, even though Granny thinks that's nonsense. Fortunately, besides the old wise doctor, a kind of itinerant preacher hangs out in the Bonhomme district. It is a certain Doekele Dykstra who presses the Frisians to get better at learning the language of the new land. Dykstra, a gung-ho Frisian himself, now and then preaches at one of their Frisian get-togethers: "When I was coming here just now, I saw quite a line-up of American cars, but as long as you don't have a decent command of English, you will never fully count."

When in the spring of 1925 twins Nammen and Lolke scurry to the wooden school on the other side of the hill, an upsetting message awaits them. The teacher stands by the door and says in English: "From now on Nammen will be called Nanno, and Lolke Lawrence!" A lifetime later, Nanno Hiemstra can still hear the teacher's announcement. "That was quite a shock, but that evening Mom said: 'Take ownership of your new name but otherwise stay who you are.'"

In March 1926 the family gets hit by tragedy. Brother Jacob, who as a boy of barely four came to America nearly naked, so to speak, loses control of horse and wagon and is killed at age nineteen. It is a blow for Douwe and Geartsje and the whole family, even though a Band-Aid is placed on the wound. On November 10 another Jacob is born. And that with Geartsje well on the way to fifty. As always, experience-expert Grandma Ytsje does not have to think long about her commentary: "Love is patient, love is kind."

It is Thursday, October 24, 1929, the day that will later be known as Black Thursday. On Wall Street the New York Stock Exchange crashes. Panic in the international financial world. It becomes clear that the economy had been heating up to excess. The first thing that father Douwe thinks of is to withdraw his money from the bank in Avon that very same Thursday. Instead of debt he now has savings in the bank after all.

Son Nanno some eighty years later: "I still remember, Lawrence and I were sitting in the back of the little Ford, we arrived at the bank and there was a piece of paper on the door – 'Closed.'"

"The bank is closed, Dad."

"Is that really what it says?"

"Yes, Dad."

"Then we're in big trouble, we'll become dirt poor." Douwe Hiemstra is so shaken, he hardly dares to drive home in his Ford.

The worst depression of the new age begins to wreak its havoc, first and most consequential in the land that is the most responsible for the collapse of the global economy. Years follow in which the farm families in the area of Springfield and Avon also suffer mercilessly under the crushing weight of disappearing means. It turns into grinding poverty. Nanno in 2012: "I was still a school boy but felt how my parents landed into terrible poverty. Dad changed into a silent, at times melancholy person – in retrospect, he suffered from depression himself; Mother fought like a tiger so to speak to be able to still take care of her family. Before this she had started to go into town with a cart to peddle cream from door to door, but no one had a penny left to spend. As a child I felt the oppressive weight of the atmosphere; Lawrence and I hardly dared to ask for something to eat. Dad and Mom had sacrificed nearly everything and crossed the ocean to make a better life. They had worked themselves to death for a better future, and now they were caught in a poverty that was even worse than that around 1885 in the Frisian countryside. I still remember, first the price of grain and milk went down, followed by a drought that scorched everything. But it got even worse: disease among the cattle and plagues in the crops that nobody could figure out. I can still see Dad walk across the yard one evening, his undershirt unbuttoned and sweat on his face."

The drought hangs on; it reaches a point where in states like Oklahoma, Nebraska, and the Dakotas not a sprig grows anymore. There are whole areas where not a drop of water falls all summer long. Such deep ruts run through the barren plains that it begins to look like the map of the United States.

If something does grow, like some leaves on a bush or tree, then the grasshoppers approach like an enormous green cloud. Whatever is left on earth to plunder is consumed in a half hour's time. And then the coup de grace is still to come: the dust storms, which are more destructive than the worst snow storm.

"The cows became so skinny, you could hang your coat on one," Nanno remembers later. "In fact, our whole family lost weight." Only now, after so many years, he dares to broach the subject. "You must not forget, for us everything was gone. If Dad and Mom had had a few pennies, they wouldn't have been able to pay for anything with them because there was nothing to buy anymore. All that was left in the end was barter. Some farmers drove with all their belongings in a ramshackle truck to the Far West. I still remember the oldest son of our neighbor Svendrup was going to do that too, but the boy apparently thought better of it, because one morning he was hanging in the barn."

Can one think of a more macabre image of the Depression? A heartbreaking funeral on the yard of the Sverre Svendrup Farm, where the dark-gray dust of the Dust Bowl covers everything.

When will the first rain shower come? It has to get worse first. Three-quarters of the herd dies from splenic fever and lung disease, and the animals that escape this death-dance contract foot-and-mouth disease. The milk cows dry up. And how did things go in the front of the farm? "At night we sometimes had a hard time getting to sleep on a half-empty stomach; we heard the barking prairie wolves come closer and closer, for those animals were running around on half empty too. Only Grandma Ytsje had an explanation: "I have to admit that we are sorely tried, but the Lord our Lord chastises those he loves."

When Nanno, as old as he's become, thinks back on his childhood years, he sees again that small group of kids of whom he was one on the way to the little wooden school. He and his twin brother Lawrence hurry along a dull-colored path; the hot prairie wind has sucked the last drop of water and the last bit of color from the wasted hill country. Mom has given a breadbox along with a piece of bread inside for each of them. Homemade bread, spread with lard – that's all. Fortunately the Federal Surplus Relief Corporation supplements it with a bit more to eat and drink at school.

"We didn't dare talk about our empty stomachs later on; we felt even as children that this was the darkest page in Mom and Dad's life." When Nanno Hiemstra at his advanced age airs the hard edge of the truth, his emotions rise to the surface.

"And then came the terrible day... That morning we were about a mile and a half on the way to school and noticed that there was something odd about the sky. At first we thought it was a thunderstorm brewing; later we figured it was a tornado. The kids wanted to hustle back home. But Lawrence and I were about eleven, twelve, and said: 'Nothing doing, the school is closest!' So we ran as fast as we could. And then, all of a sudden, it became dark from the dust storm. If there hadn't been a barbed wire strung along the school path, we would've completely lost our way. Fortunately our teacher pulled us one by one into the schoolhouse.

For a little while it got a bit lighter, but then the wind kicked up and then it became really as dark as night.

'A tornado after all' – the teacher let the words escape. Lawrence and I knew what a tornado was, so we were already under the bench. 'Let us pray that it isn't a tornado,' said Lawrence, and we prayed, and then it became obvious that it wasn't a tornado but the Great Dust Bowl. 'It's only dust,' the teacher called out. But there was no end to it; we could already write our names in the dust on the school benches. It went on and on, and then the door sprung open and someone stumbled into the room. Completely covered with dust, he looked like the devil himself. I saw that he had blood on his hands and that tears were rolling down his blackened cheeks.

'Dad!' Lawrence cried. And it was our dad! Nearly blind from the dust, Dad had followed the barbed wire fence. He wanted to find out if we had made it safe and sound to the school. If I remember right, Dad and us made it home that night just before bedtime.

Mom had put the plates upside down on the table, otherwise we would have had to eat more dust porridge than corn porridge. 'Let's pray!' commanded Grandma. 'Lord bless this food, Amen.' I still remember, it was porridge made from the last bit of corn, the syrup had been gone for a few weeks already."

The day comes when their last work horse succumbs to a mysterious illness. The animal had stood sleeping for a few days already, and now it collapses and is near death. Veterinarian Ebbing is certain that the poisonous Russian yellow star thistle is the cause. The horses are hungry too, of course, and can't leave the thistles alone. The shriveled-up plants blow like bouncing balls across the dried-out prairie.

"We've lost nearly everything now," repeats Douwe Hiemstra. Grandma's Bible texts have for the moment been exhausted, but she does make her statement: "When everything is nearly gone, there must still be something left!"

Nanno, much later: "I felt the tension. Dad, humiliated, stared in the distance. In retrospect, I saw his vulnerability for the first time then. He sat, bent down – like later Marinus van der Lubbe did in Hitler's famous propaganda photograph – and wanted just one thing: to return! Back to Hichtum. But he knew at the same time that his precious other half had suffered a trauma during the terrible journey in February of 1911. Mother simply could not go back."

In the icy winter of the Depression year 1934, Grandma Ytsje Namminga-Wytsma begins to fail; soon she can't be on her feet anymore. She knows right away that this will not pass. On the bright, frosty, early afternoon of February 11 she hums the sacred Evensong for the last time. She doesn't miss a word. The room is crowded with her descendants, young and older. Her deathbed stands in the corner. "The journey was difficult, but the arrival will make up for it all." No, Grandma Ytsje in this cruel world does not lose her way, not even at the end, though she thinks for a moment that she is back in the stately town with the stubby tower. Names are dropped of people who stayed behind, a flight of birds flies overhead one of them of another kind, a very special specimen. On February 13, 1934, in the darkest days of the Depression, Ytsje Namminga-Wytsma passes on at age 83. A few days later she is entrusted to the soil of her Land of Deliverance.

After that winter, spring follows again, and a summer, and a fall, and a long winter, and then at last some improvement comes. The American government provides the country farmers with wheat meal which they can pick up from the train depot in Springfield. Call it what it is: the fight against hunger. 'Supplemental feeding,' Douwe Hiemstra calls it. For a couple of dollars pay, the farmers may help plant trees and convert mud paths to gravel roads, all of this to prevent erosion in times of drought and dust storms.

The Hiemstras regain courage. Nanno can harness a couple of fresh horses to the wagon again. In the meanwhile he's become a young man of seventeen and an expert with horses. Who is better with horses than David and Gertrude's Nanno from the Hiemstra Farm? He takes responsibility for the transportation of the wheat meal. Later on he also takes on the transportation of gravel for hardening the roads. He hauls the gravel from the railway and takes it to the far corners of the county, all the way to McGlenehens Pit and Jensma's Pit. Fourteen hours a day in motion, then there's still an eight-hour night left. Once a week he treats himself to a hot dog along the way.

"I had my eye on Alice Coehoorn, met her at the youth society behind the church, and for some time already I couldn't keep my eyes off her. Not that it matters, but she was also the cutest girl of all of Bonhomme." She was born as Aaltsje in Iowa; her folks had come from Rotstergaast in 1918, "from the Tsjonger River Side," after they had landed there in bitter poverty in the depression years around 1884.

Nanno began to realize around 1940 that farming in the Dakotas was risky. "'Dad, we should leave here; let's rent a place in Washington State, California, or Wisconsin. The land is more productive there, not too dry, fewer tornadoes.' But Dad and Mom turned out to be attached to the land that had treated them so cruelly. I couldn't understand that initially, but I can now: Jacob's grave, that's what they were attached to."

Later, when Nanno hears that there's a great farm for rent near Sharon in Wisconsin, father Douwe travels over there to have a look.

"It's not bad," he says when home again. In fact he is pretty excited about it. "I kind of think that we should do it." Son Nanno under-stands the language of his father David's heart.

On Wednesday, October 15, 1941, all is ready for the move to Wisconsin. Exodus by train. In Springfield, five train cars stand ready, loaded with milk cows, heifers, a couple of horse teams, a stallion, farm implements, equipment, tools, and furniture. A cou-ple of hammocks are strung among the animals for Nanno and his younger brother David. But there won't be much sleeping in the coming days – the men will be too busy milking, cleaning, feeding, and tending. The drinking water first comes from the Missouri, lat-er from the Upper Mississippi. And so they rumble through South Dakota, a tip of Iowa, right through Minnesota, and after that a ways into Wisconsin. For the last couple of miles the cattle have to be driven to the farm. With the final destination in sight, there is still a wooden dam; they practically have to lift the cattle over it one by one, but the exodus finally reaches its conclusion.

On December 5 in the same year of 1941 St. Nicholas Eve is cele-brated in a new, comfortable farm near Sharon. The voice of Grand-ma Ytsje can still be heard… "Grandma would say, 'The crisis has passed, good, a Second World War has taken its place, but that's happening on the other side of the ocean.'"

Two days after the St. Nicholas celebration the Japanese attack Pearl Harbor; WWII has now started for the Americans too. Only nine days later they've located Nanno in the village of Sharon, WI. He's dressed in his old overalls with patches over the knees, compliments of Grandma Ytsje, when the mailman personally hands him the draft notice for military service. It's as if Nanno is literally torn from his farmer's life. "I already have to have my physical."

There's no reason for 6'3" athletic Nanno not to pass his physical. That's also true for his twin brother who stayed behind in South Dakota, but Lawrence gets an exemption. Not only because he's fifteen minutes younger than Nanno, but because he has a wife and farm. Now that the country is at war, farming becomes a kind of war industry.

Nanno Hiemstra travels by train to the training camp, Camp Barkley in Texas, after which he's assigned to the 90th Infantry Division of the Third American Army that later in Europe will fall under General George Patton's command. The young men begin to realize that a different set of concerns is now awaiting them. The military training is tough as nails and long. Nanno and Alice look each other in the eyes and decide to get married. He is 21 now, she almost two years younger.

For the first time in her life, Alice gets on the train to catch up with her husband in Texas – two days of travel to Camp Barkley. Why wouldn't there be work for her in the barracks? But no, there's nothing. Well, then maybe get to work as a cotton picker, if that pays well enough. Poverty and diligence, she's grown up with that. But one thing is certain: the two are infinitely happy, and they want to make a future together as farmers.

Life goes on till a telegram reaches them from Wisconsin. Nanno's older brother Charles has unexpectedly died from an internal hemorrhage. Nanno and Alice decide to take a train back to Sharon, WI immediately. In Camp Barkley his buddies hold a collection to contribute to the travel expenses for the young couple. Two days later they stand by the grave of the brother who was also their best friend. Beside them a young mother with two small children. Next to them his deeply grieving parents who for the third time must bury a child: first their twins in Hichtum, then a grown son

100

in Avon, SD, and now again a wonderful boy who already had a family.

And then, that same evening, a farewell at the little station of Sharon, WI. Mother says: "And now you have to cross the ocean soon to fight to your death."

"No, Mom, I promise that I will come back."

Nanno and Alice are back in Texas, later travel to California where Nanno receives a year-long, very intense additional training. With a soldier's and cotton picker's pay they cannot afford a house right away.

At the beginning of March 1944, Nanno finds out that he will be shipped out to an unknown destination. First he can go on leave, back with Alice to Wisconsin. Then on to the war.

Goodbyes at the small station of Sharon. "I pressed myself to Alice's bulging belly. 'Can you feel the baby?' she wanted to know. 'Yes,' I said, 'I can feel it move.' She had been expecting for seven, eight months already.

And then, at a short distance, I saw Dad and Mom standing there, crying, holding hands."

Like Father...

Johannes Boorsma has gained a cruel enemy; his thriving Bicycle Sales and Repair Shop has been hit by the depression of the 1930s. "The dumbest farmer suddenly discovered that he's smart enough to fix a flat tire himself." When Johannes vents with these outbursts, his displeasure is tangible. "Stop!" He snarls more and more. "I will no longer be taunted with 'the Kaiser,' for the kaisers and kings in Europe have had their time. Long live the People's Republic."
Lately he often stops at the Swan café on the Tow Road in Workum, and there they know him only as the Kaiser. His outspoken commentary on the affairs of the world booms through the room.

"Hell yes, it's a depression!" The main culprits are the American money sharks. According to Johannes they let the stock markets and banks collapse. They let the whole economy go to pot, with the result that the farmer gets less than a nickel for two pints of milk. "It's bad in Germany too, the Germans have to pay through the nose for their so-called war debt: to the French, the English who in Africa confine the Boers behind barbed wire, and now also to the Americans, because dammit, they make life miserable for the Germans too."

"How do you know all that, Kaiser? And what do you have against my three brothers in America!"

"Hey, hey, no fighting here." Tension rises in the taproom of the Swan, but Johannes marches on: "The Americans did not get their land honestly, they grabbed it from the Native Indians and afterward murdered them. That's terrible! That's even worse than how the Dutch landlords abuse us as sharecroppers. Don't you see how they pull the wool over our eyes? The big shots want to keep us poor and dumb and docile. And you know what? They're succeeding." And then Johannes ends his tirade with: "Those who turn themselves into sheep will be eaten by wolves."

It finally comes down to the fact that the Bicycle Sales and Repair Shop is barely making it. In the twenties the pace was still steady, but since the dry summer and the three fall storms of 1928 it's been trouble. Not that the people of Workum and surroundings had much awareness that right after Thursday, October 24 – Black Thursday – the stock market collapsed here too. There had been a winter, and they had felt that. The winter of 1929.

It became icy cold. Johannes and Pytsje could barely keep the stove burning. The whole month of February they sat close to the stove in their coats. The frozen canal between Workum and Bolsward creaked with frost; it became quiet on the country roads. Johannes kept busy with varnishing a decent second-hand work bike. Before long you couldn't tell it from a new one. And he gave his showpiece the trade name of 'Karst Leemburg.' For wasn't it this day laborer who on February 12 swished past the houseboat, a strapping young man? At Nijhuzum Leemburg caught up with the breakaway racers, and in long sweeping strokes he showed them how it is done. It was a case of 'get them and over them'; Karst Leemburg left everyone behind.

Johannes had seen his hero skate, and had deep respect for the man he regarded as his partner in misfortune, the day laborer who became the champion in the Eleven-City Race of 1929.

That very same week the trumpets would blare in the Swan: "In exchange for a frozen toe, eternal fame for a poor son of a gun who proved that the little guy can rise above the big shot Dutchmen. Dammit, do you agree with me or not! Whoever is oppressed here shall from now on show his mettle. Look at Germany! There the common people will take power into their own hands."

"Cheers. To the Kaiser."

The thirties arrive. When on May 12, 1930 socialist, poet, anti-monarchist, and Member of Parliament Piter Jelles Troelstra passes away, Johannes Boorsma gives free rein to his emotions. "Right after the First World War we let our Piter Jelles down for good, and now we'll pay the price*. Then we could have rescued ourselves from the royal clique with Piter Jelles as leader, like the Germans rescued themselves from the Kaiser clique. But no, we turned ourselves into sheep again. And now we have to comply with a gold thief like conservative Prime Minister Colijn."

"Cheers."

"To the Kaiser."

Johannes's oldest son Meindert years later will put it this way: "I was eleven and Dad wanted to take me along to the funeral of Piter Jelles Troelstra, but this time he hadn't reckoned with Mom. Sensible as she was, she was able to talk Dad out of this cross-country trip. The Enclosure Dam wasn't there yet."

When young Meindert Boorsma comes home during school time with the announcement that he no longer wants to go to school, Dad's anger explodes. "Back to school, right now, you lunkhead!" Dad, just back from the Swan, forgets to ask the reason for Meindert's announcement.

In the Workum schoolyard his son was tagged as "the son of the Kaiser from the little houseboat." Time and again he had to defend himself and his brother and sisters till blood flowed. With both fists. That morning before school started his attackers drove him into the corner of the schoolyard, and when he had finally fought himself free, he saw the school principal standing motionless in the school door. At that moment Meindert made up his mind.

"No, I'm never going back to school. Never! I can take care of myself." He's not going to humiliate himself by telling his parents about the taunting and the bullying.

"You will do what I say!" Now he feels the point of his dad's wood-

---

* In November of 1918 Troelstra tried, but failed to overthrow the monarchy and establish a socialist republic modeled on the Russian Revolution. He did not get the support of the working class he had anticipated.

en shoe, and Dad kicks hard. Meindert does not buckle under, stays standing, fearless and straight. It's that posture that makes his dad furious. His voice changing pitch, he comes toward the boy: "You're smart and you will study. If not, then I'll teach you something."

"Go ahead, just kick me to death! Go ahead, Dad, kill me. Because I will never, never again go to school!"

A sensible mother jumps in between. "That's enough, Dad, the boy is upset." The dad calms down.

"They want to keep our kind of people dumb." Johannes Boorsma breathes heavily and his words come out hoarse. "And this way they're going to succeed too. Because, dammit, we don't have enough education. As a kid my dad gathered shitty tufts of sheep wool to stay alive and for all that I sat under a cow when I was only twelve. And then I recently had to place our own daughter, our Lysbeth of twelve, with a farmer. My child in a cow barn bed with manure on its doors. Isn't an end to this slavery ever going to come?"

The dad turns back to his son and says, now more quietly: "I'm willing to crawl on my knees, boy, if you'll go to school and get an education."

"I don't want Dad to crawl for me, I want to take care of myself."

"Can't you get it through your head then that knowledge is power?"

"I don't need power!" The boy is shouting now. "When ten big boys together want to beat me up, there's no use." The boy rushes out, grabs his leaping pole from the flat roof, takes a run-up, leaps across the canal and heads for the fields, in search of freedom, justice, and work. Yes, work, for he's not afraid of that. At work, he can be anybody's equal.

The dad stares after his son in confusion. His Kaiser-like mustache has changed in the meantime to the one of the man who in Germany is rising on the firmament as the new Führer. He leaves on his re-varnished work bike, and it knows the path to café the Swan.

When his son comes home around bedtime, a mother stands in

the door trembling with worry, waiting for him. She lets him in without saying a word. It turns out that Dad has hauled the school principal to the Bicycle Sales and Repair Shop. Pale, the principal of the school faces Johannes Boorsma.

"Here he is! Our boy. You have the floor, teacher." The teacher promises that he will not allow a throng to push Meindert into a corner of the schoolyard. And the teacher will also see to it that the children in school and on the schoolyard will no longer bully him by calling him Meindert Kaiser.

"You don't have to say any more," the pupil responds, "I just got a job as junior farm helper with Tsjipke Goslinga. The boss said that I can take side-lessons in Parregea. For the rest I can take of myself."

On an early and dark morning in November 1930 he goes along with his dad to catch golden plovers with a clapnet on the Heidenskip Commons.

"It's pretty darn cold, Dad."

"A plover catcher has to think himself warm."

Pretty soon Dad hauls out his lure whistle, is going to blow on it, changes his mind and says: "No one has ever been able to imitate a bird as well as your grandpa. They called your grandpa Meindert Birdie."

"I know that, there was somebody at school who teased me with 'Birdie.'"

"That's nothing to be ashamed of, it's a title of honor. You didn't know your grandpa, but I'm telling you, the man in his youth carved a bird whistle out of a cow bone and dolled it up with little copperplates and it became a miraculous instrument. When it was finished, he could imitate any meadow bird, and so amazingly beautiful and realistic that the birds thought of him as a bird."

"What happened to Grandpa's first bird whistle?" The boy wants to know.

"He made more than one," the father says evasively.

"Where is it?"

106

"That whistle belongs with the soul of your grandpa, and where his soul is now… I can tell you this, it is buried with my dad."

"Grandpa wanted to travel with the birds to faraway lands, but he thought that then he would have to leave his soul behind. In his heart he wanted to go to America, but because of that he held back. Dad would have liked to go to America too, but because Grandpa didn't go, you stayed here too."

"How would you know that, you monkey head."

"I know it from Grandma Willemke. Every time I was staying with her, she told me about Grandpa Birdie."

It's quiet for a long time, then the boy says: "When I'm grown up, I'll travel anywhere."

"Then you should know that in a flight of plovers, sometimes a bird travels with them to comfort others. One who undertakes a long journey needs comfort."

"Mom is my comfort bird. For the rest I'll take care of myself."

The cold fall has removed all color and sound from the Heidenskip Commons; in the hazy distance not a bird can be seen or heard. The father digs in the inside pocket of his heavy overcoat and hands a plover whistle to Meindert. The boy kneels and blows and plays on it with closed eyes. The father listens and hears his dad. When the boy says a bit later that he hasn't succeeded in thinking himself warm, the father tells him to come and sit closer to him.

It's been a long time since the son felt his dad's warmth. After a while Meindert says: "Before Grandpa died, Grandma Willemke had to promise that she had to tell me everything about Grandpa."

"When Grandpa died, you still had to be born."

"That's exactly why, he knew that I was going to be born."

"Oh you darn rascal – you're so serious, call the plovers once more. Come on, whistle like you did a while ago."

"Dad, you know this too, the plover really has to call the birder first, then the birder can answer and lure and catch."

Behind them the noise of the cane beetle from the Fluezen invades the silence; the boy listens and listens. After some fifteen minutes he hears something. It is no more than a high musical note, a light touch of the bow on the string of the violin, a cry as if from a helpless soul in his last hour.

"Dad, I heard something!" The boy feels tension in the father's belly wedged tight against him, sees right in front of his eyes a pair of old eyes drowned in cold tears, and in a weathered fist the plover whistle. The father places the whistle to his mouth, hesitates for a second, then whistles. The boy sees a heavy forefinger dance, and thinks of the man he's never known, but whom he thinks he loves more than his own dad.

Dad calls, but gets no answer.

"Here, let me give you a plug of tobacco, you're old enough now to learn to chew. What? Bitter? What in the world, I wasn't yet twelve when I already kept my wad inside my school desk." Meindert pushes a few threads behind his teeth and has to do his best not to gag on them.

They're there till three in the afternoon, then he can't resist any longer: "I'd like to go home."

"Not yet, it's going to get dusky pretty soon and then the worms in the sod of the commons are going to go into action, and if the plovers are around then, we can expect them here."

Dad's last lure call sounds like a lamentation.

It is the boy who hears something. "Dad, they're coming." And then the father lets the decoys dance to the tune the boy is singing. A flight of plovers, some twenty of them, flies like a whirlwind through the treetops over their screen.

"They're coming back." Johannes Boorsma is already bending deeply at the pull cord, with the other hand letting the decoys dance on a fine string. "Now!" A little ahead of them the bird net comes down in full force. Most of the birds escape, but several golden plovers a bit later have to yield themselves to human hands. Fifty yards ahead a large water plover lies motionless on the ground. "He must've flown right through the net," the father decides.

"The plover wanted only to do good, but had to pay for it with his death," the boy says.

He's hardly twelve when he becomes the resident junior farmhand on Tsjipke Goslinga's big farm below Parregea. Meindert is a precocious boy. Handy and tough as nails. Now and then he works with the steady farmhand. His wages: a hundred and fifty guilders per year with room and board. Ordinarily the farmer pays out the wages at the end of the year, but without him asking for it, Goslinga pays Meindert seventy-five guilders after a few weeks, and on top of that adds a second-hand bike in good shape. "Now you can visit your mom more often in the houseboat." There's no mention of Dad, but Meindert can tell by the smell of the oil on the chain that the farmer ordered the bike from the Bicycle Sales and Repairs Shop.

It's St. Nicholas Eve 1931. The household of Johannes and Pytsje Boorsma now looks like this: Lysbeth of fourteen and a farmer's maid in Ferwâlde for a couple of years already; Meindert twelve and farmhand below Parregea; Willemke eleven; Albert six, and Pytsje four years old. Meindert will cherish the St. Nicholas celebration of 1931 as a warm memory till his death. "Well, yes, the only regrettable thing was that my younger brother Albert was sickly; the whooping cough went around in the Workum area."

Less than a week later Johannes Boorsma appears at Goslinga's in the cow barn during milking time. "Meindert!" His dad has taken his cap off. "Can you leave that cow for a minute?" There stands the junior farmhand, now as tall as his dad, and he sees that Dad's mouth is trembling. "Our Albert has died."

The junior farmhand stands there, numb, in one hand a bucketful of milk and in the other the milk stool. In the semi-darkness, the farmer makes his appearance. He lays his hand on the father's shoulder, and Meindert – still with milk bucket and stool – is suddenly attacked by an irrational rage: "Boss, keep your hands off my dad!"

After the death of Albert, the luster of life is gone in and around the Bicycle Sales and Repair Shop.

A NAZI SYMPATHIZER

"Meindert, you're turning into quite a young man, you should become a member of the NSB* like your dad!" The encouragement comes from farm wife Tryntsje Deddes, the wife of Rintsje Haagsma, born in 1890, stockbreeder on the Tow Road in Workum. Haagsma and his wife don't just say it, they shout it from the rooftop. On the black roof tiles of the barn red letters proclaim: 'N S B', letters large enough for people in Parregea, two miles away, to read.

"I'm not doing anything, Mrs. Haagsma!" Meindert doesn't want to belong to anything. He adds for Mrs. Haagsma's ears that his dad is not so fond of NSB chairman Mussert: "That guy, according to my dad, shows off too much when he sings our national anthem".

The Depression takes its toll; there's massive unemployment. Those who still have work, like in the work relief program, earn very little and are often forced to sleep in barracks for a week. Farmers who farm with borrowed money, secured by relatives or friends, and who because of the low milk price go broke, drag their guarantors into misery with them. This gives cause to unbearable tensions among families everywhere. Those who prize their status often cannot bear their loss and shame, and thus end their life.

The analysis of Johannes Boorsma in the Swan: "It won't be much longer until a farmer will hang from every Frisian tree."

Even Tsjipke Goslinga, who like so many farmers leans toward Germany and for the rest waits to see what will happen, gets an earful from Johannes. And that on an afternoon when the man comes down to pay off the second-hand bike. Goslinga: "This past winter,

---

* The Nationaal Socialistische Beweging, the Dutch National Socialist Movement, which sympathized with Hitler.

below Wergea, a Hornstra and his wife roped themselves together and skated into an ice hole on the Wergea Canal. Skating together toward death, both pitifully drowned. Can you think of anything worse!"

"Yes, I can!" Johannes explodes with a curse. Was it the drink in the Swan?

"The farmer and his wife in the wetlands below Wergea made that choice themselves. But an innocent child, that is smothered in his last sickness and dies, he didn't make that choice! Shall I tell you something? That wetlands farmer and his wife didn't get along, they didn't trust each other, both thought: I'm going to tie you to me. If I'm going to go in, then you will too."

Goslinga lets it go: you can't get anywhere with the Kaiser lately.

As the thirties go by and there are mutterings about a war-minded Germany, resentment and distrust become more and more prevalent. Meindert now and then feels that his dad gives him the cold shoulder; then he's the Kaiser's boy again. As a live-in farmhand he has an excellent place on the farm of Harmen and Sytske Posthumus in the Tsjerkwert hamlet of Iemswâlde. According to Meindert, war will never happen here. In the meanwhile he's become a senior farmhand of eighteen, almost 6'3", strong as an ox, and entrusted with all kinds of farm work. The work comes easy to him: he's both handy and quick.

"Those were good years in that small community," he will often say later. Posthumus also had a permanent worker: Douwe Tjittes Wyngaarden from Tsjerkwert. And then in Iemswâlde there was among others the cute and charming Kûbaard milk hauler's daughter Jetske Hiemstra. She's a farmer's maid on a farm about seven hundred feet farther on.

Meindert and Jetske fall in love, dream of better times, of a good-looking modest laborer's home with a chicken run, a nice household, freedom, a permit to catch birds.

In the late winter of 1939-1940 Posthumus says to Meindert: "The milk price is still so-so; coming May I won't be able to hang on to both of you."

"Then I will look for another spot by Alde Maaie 1940." Meindert is decisive, knows that Douwe has a household, and thinks that he has to give up his place for that. But it is mobilization time; a few days later Douwe Wyngaarden gets the call that he has to go back into military service. The threat of war has become all too real, even in Iemswâlde, and therefore Meindert can stay living with Harm and Sytske Posthumus.

May 10, 1940, at a quarter past four in the morning, Meindert is milking a cow in the milk yard with his sight toward the east. And there it rises: a majestic sun which separates itself like an egg from stepmother earth. A new day.

"How is it going at this moment with Douwe in the trenches at the Grebbeberg?" he wonders. "Everything is so weird and meaningless here," Douwe had scribbled in very small letters on a picture postcard.

Right through the sound of the spurts in the milk bucket another sound is audible; it is a droning high in the sky. Surely not airplanes? In a milk yard farther on someone shouts: "It is war, I heard it on the radio myself!" Meindert stares into the heavens, sees airplanes like flights of plovers flying to the southwest.

In the milk yard the farmers keep milking. Cannons may roar, wounds bleed, but when the cow releases its milk, the milking must be done. And when it's growing season, the mowing must be done.

When the milking is finished and the breakfast table ready, the milk hauler says to Johannes Kaiser's Meindert as he passes by him: "And you, Meindert, just tell that German old man of yours that he betrayed the crap out of us." With that it becomes clear to Meindert what kind of position he can expect in the next little while.

The Pentecost holidays are coming up, and Meindert and Jetske have been planning for the last six months that they will enjoy two days off together. First on the bike to her folks, then stop by the houseboat below Nijhuzum, and then together to the Ryster Forest. But when he arrives to pick her up, she acts very dismissively. Why, in heaven's name? That evening he tries once more, but now she won't even make an appearance.

It's as if the ground disappears beneath him; it feels as if they once again pushed him into the corner of the schoolyard, making him desperate. He had always been able to fight himself free, but this war is already lost. His confusion and uncertainty turn into panic. He has to get out of here, but where to? To Mom in the houseboat? To the Goslingas? No, he must now speak to Jetske face to face.

"What's wrong? Say it to my face then. Did I start this war? Does my whole life have to go to hell then?" That's what he wants to say to her. But he changes his mind; he's not going to crawl for anyone, not even for her with whom he's so in love. Meindert, my man, he says to himself, go to your mom, you not only need her but she needs you too.

"As you know, I was going to take the holidays off," he says to the farmer as he takes his leave.

"But Meindert my boy, it is war. At the head of the Enclosure Dam they're fighting to the death." And the farmer's wife adds: "Douwe's at the Grebbeberg already, pretty soon you too will become cannon fodder."

"Tuesday morning at four o'clock I'll be back at it," he says.

With the leaping pole on his shoulder he wanders through the fields, avoids the paved roads. Along the uncertain path between peace and war. It takes him past Jonkershuzen, Arkum, Dedzjum, Hieslum, and on to Nijhuzum. Even from a distance he sees on the farm of Rintsje Haagsma the red, white and blue of the Dutch flag wave above the large letters 'N S B'.

No flag on the houseboat. Dad, his eyes gleaming in victory, stands in the houseboat door, not in euphoria but sure enough in his new suit. Clean-shaven, white collar, wearing a tie, the mustache – graying a bit – neatly trimmed.

"They're here," he calls out. "They asked for this in The Hague*, but don't worry, not a sparrow will fall, Friesland has already surrendered."

Meindert goes to his mother, who keeps herself deep inside the houseboat. "Mom, it's all over," he says.

"It is war," he repeats, "it's all over."

And on the road ahead of him, from the direction of Bolsward, hundreds of armed Germans approach, in a relaxed march. With horse and wagon, cars, small artillery, armed vehicles, and a soldier on motorbike zooming around the whole procession. At the Nijhuzum Bridge the Wehrmacht sings, and on the side of the Tow Road Johannes Boorsma sings along:

"Es ist so schön Soldat zu sein, Rosemarie
Nicht jeder Tag bringt Sonnenschein, Rosemarie
Doch du, du bist mein Talisman, Rosemarie
Du gehest im allen mir voran, Rosemarie
Soldaten sind Soldaten
Im Worten und im Taten
Sie kennen keine Lumperei
Und sind nur einem Mädel treu
Vellari, Valleralle ralle ra!"

[It's so good to be a soldier, Rosemarie
Not every day brings sunshine, Rosemarie
But you, you are my talisman, Rosemarie
You lead the way in everything, Rosemarie
Soldiers are soldiers
In words and in deeds
They know no Raggamuffinhood

---

* The Hague is the Dutch seat of government.

And are true to one girl
Valleri, Valleralle ralle ra!]

A good week later. No shots are fired anymore. The Netherlands capitulates. Douwe Wyngaarden returns from the Grebbeberg battle front, a bit more confused and quiet than he was already. Meindert has to help him twice out of the ditch because he thought that he was under fire. A few days later Douwe says: "I think I'm able to go on again."

When sometime later on a Saturday evening, the farmer gives each of them an extra couple of guilders because of the rise in the price of milk, Meindert quits his job with the words: "There is no place here for me anymore." He can no longer stomach the fact that in the milk yard the milkers position themselves under their cow in such a way that they don't have to see Meindert.

The day is ending. "I don't think that you'll get work." Here and there a warning follows him. He mounts his bike and leaves the neighborhood. When he bikes past the yard of her parents, he sees Jetske Hiemstra sneak into the barn. He has resigned himself and keeps pedaling on his heavily loaded bike. The sun sinks down, not a creature is heard anymore, not a hand waves goodbye.

The next day, Sunday morning at ten o'clock, he takes his leave from his parents and sisters in the houseboat. A day later at Coevorden, at four o'clock in the morning, he also takes leave of the land of his citizenship. Three times he's stopped, and each time he successfully hauls out his dad's Addressenbuch [address book] and nice Prüfungzeugnissen [certificates]. Yes, he's biking into Germany to get a milking job. A day later, just before bedtime, he arrives at Hermann Girke's farm, an invalid, in the town of Hollenbeck, not far from Muenster.

"Donnerwetter!" The crippled farmer exclaims, "this Meinhart looks just like his dad Johannes!" There are so many sons under arms that there is a howling shortage of milkers. That damn war. Yes, his dad Johannes was a fantastic milker, Girke beams. "Like father, like son?"

A month and a half later he can send a comforting letter home, with a hundred Marks enclosed. 'For Mother'. He does that almost every other month, until they do not hear from him anymore in the houseboat.

One evening Meindert Boorsma is caught by the police while he's secretly listening to a British radio station. They suspect him to be a spy, and he lands in a cell on Hindenburgstrasse 78 in Muenster. All he needs to do is say 'yes,' but he keeps insisting that he's not a spy. Endless days and nights follow with brutal interrogations, until he's ready to climb the walls.

One night a somewhat older military man comes and says calmly and convincingly: "You are free, my boy, we will put you on the train tomorrow morning, then you can go see your parents in Friesland. All set! All you need to do is sign this paper." He signs.

The next day he's indeed on the train. Destination: the training camp of the Waffen SS near Graz in Austria. By sheer coincidence he manages to avoid getting his blood type tattooed on his under-arm, but the SS-sign is tattooed in his left arm pit.

THE LIBERATOR

On the fourth story of the Chicago Grand Railroad Office, Nanno finds a small table for himself. He and another couple of hundred thousand American military personnel were just informed that after this there will be no communication possible at all with the home front. "Time to say goodbye," he hears all around him. But what does that mean in the old language of Dad and Mom? Write a letter first to Alice. No, better write the old folks first. A few sentences, which will long be saved, first in a small drawer in his parents' house, later in his own drawer that he will not often open:

> [...] Whatever will happen to me, what I took with me from
> my parents is worth more than gold. That's what makes the
> writing of these lines so difficult. What is precious to you
> is hard to let go. I promise dad and mom that I will do my
> best to come back safe and sound. [...]

At the end of March 1944, as a part of an endless column of soldiers with heavy backpacks, he steps onto the gangway of the English tanker Ethicon Castle. By this time Nanno Hiemstra has been in service for two years already. And it has hardly been a picnic. After Camp Barkley they were sent to Louisiana for more advanced training. At times it became so brutal that some five men died. After that they set off to California for even more advanced military exercises. Sometimes it seemed like a real war, which revolted him.

So all these men now embarking are not exactly ignorant simpletons about the war ahead of them. Each can sense that it's going to turn into a spectacular attack on the European coastline. Where exactly that's going to happen and when, remains the question. The Ethicon Castle, loaded as it is with gasoline as well as infantry in every nook and cranny, makes for a vulnerable target for German

U-boats and bombers. They've chosen as much as possible a north-erly route across the Atlantic. Besides, they're sailing in convoy formation. The weather is stormy. March showers, a rough sea, icy cold. Circling the convoy is a swarm of speedy destroyer escorts and frigates armed with torpedoes to keep the German submarines at bay. And they have all they can handle. Just the same, the convoy is able to maintain an average speed of twelve knots an hour.

When he recalls this voyage later, he smells vomit and at times the sweat of fear; if it isn't his own nausea and fear, then surely that of his buddies. Behind him in the convoy, a ship is hit, that's certain, but the details? No information. The voyage takes twelve days and nights. The only thing they know at its end is that it's April 5 and that they've dropped anchor somewhere. When it becomes light, the contours of a harbor city appear. Liverpool. Nanno Hiemstra does not yet know at this point that while on the northern Atlantic Ocean, he became the Dad of a healthy baby girl.

"Where's a barber around here?" He hears a buddy calling. "They've thought of everything but they forgot about the barber." Nanno decides quickly: "Just come over here, I have experience with shearing sheep, I'll give you a cut and a shave for three dollars, and you may keep the tail." Ten customers amounts to thirty dollars; he dreams for the umpteenth time that he and his wife are farming a 90-acre farm, and a little boy is playing in the yard. Or a girl. God knows.

In the second half of May 1944, hundreds and hundreds of boats lie anchored in Liverpool and Cardiff, but also in many other British and Irish harbors, and a hundred thousand soldiers are ready to do what will be asked of them. And the materiel; one morning, just like that and especially for him, there is his loyal brother-in-arms of iron and steel: a thirteen-ton M5 Caterpillar truck Diamond T, and coupled behind it a piece of artillery of 105mm and a weight of six ton. He's to boss that around as long as the war shall last. He's practiced with such a behemoth for longer than a year, till he could handle it as easily as a pair of horses in front of his wheat meal- and gravel-wagon in South Dakota. Another friend joins him who introduces himself as Doug. He will be his riding mate.

"Come on, buddy. Go!"

"Yep, Wisconsin!"

"The hell. I'm from Nebraska!" They shake hands. Two pairs of hard laborer hands.

One evening under dark weather it looks like it's going to happen. Well yes, but then what? The day was already so long, now the night is likely to be long too. But then comes the command that everything – but what? – is going to be postponed. A few days later they have to line up again. This time it appears to be a go. Nanno embarks with throngs of others on a ship without a name. It's as if everything that will participate in this ultimate operation has turned in its name.

Five thousand ships with a hundred thousand heavily armed men; twenty thousand pieces of heavy equipment; a thousand parachutists who – for all anybody knows – are already in the air somewhere over enemy territory; hundreds and hundreds of airplanes, waiting somewhere for a signal from higher up to take off; gigantic battleships which soon will emerge from behind the scenes and storm ahead into the battle to unload their firepower. Nanno, are you ready for all that? Pretty soon you will have to try to make it through the surf to the beach with your Cat. Father and Mother's land?

The anchors are raised, they rush eastward in the dark night, then southeast. "If only the wheels touch the ground, then the engine isn't going to stall," Doug tries to convince himself. Doug is already at war. Against his seasickness. "If only we get ground under our wheels."

The night and the journey last an eternity. Or does it just feel that way? Can time indeed stand still? "Now we've sailed for so long already," Doug observes, "we may not be on the way to France or so but likely to the south to Italy. Rome, Naples."

"Just go to sleep, buddy!"

Another eternity later. He thinks he sees to the side of them just over port a slice of a new day coming. "That's got to be east."

"Hell, my pack of cigarettes got soaked."

"You know very well, buddy, you're not supposed to..." Nanno has hardly said the words when the earth turns into hell. Light that's unbearable to look at rises from the cellars of the sea, all begins to shake, his body, his ship, the sea, even the sky. The cannons roar, everything that can unload fire, unloads fire. Everywhere – in front, on the sides, behind him – there's light; around him he sees hundreds of ships advance, with a wrathful foaming of the mouth. Far ahead of him a coastline that begins to light up as in a raging thunderstorm; arcs of fire sail from behind over the enormous fleet to the front and land on the continent of which Dad and Mom still bear the joys and sorrows.

"Our battleships behind us are letting them have it," Doug hollers with a catch in his voice, "and why not, it's the Texas and the Nevada. My God, go at it, boys, give them hell!"

"Why," Nanno will say later, "why should I try to describe these hellish hours for someone else? How do you report what really happened on that strip of Normandy which will enter history as Utah Beach? Those hours, days, months afterward..."

Yes, he has to get the Cat and trailer over a steel flap out of the ship into the surf. With all the racket he can't even hear the running of the engine, but he does give it the pedal. The Cat is not moving, isn't touching the ground, threatens to tilt, first left, then toward the right. Will he have to drown then, at the last moment? Steel bounces against steel, it is as if the Cat is shot awake, it's 'bam!' And again, 'bam!'

"We hit ground," Doug screams. Another fierce thrust, falters, gets traction. Then an all-blinding blow, a feeling of deafness. Sand, spouting high from the beach. "Go, go!" All the horror around him, what he has to drive through and over, oh God, this can't be happening.

"Don't hit me, don't hit me!" Nanno screams inside. He advances falteringly, toward an elevation, till the Cat with howitzer runs stuck in the loose sand of the steep dune. "Doug, I'm not dead, I'm not dead! Doug, where are you hanging out!" He stares at the place where his buddy had just been sitting. Two holes in the seat, some blood and bone fragments, that's all. He sees that the right door with the white star is totally gone.

They fight their way over a hill, a day later through a valley. In front of him passes the stretcher with the boy who in the morning, right in front of him, had been holding a mug of cold coffee in a shaky hand and had lost his voice. Wasn't able to find cover in time.

For the 90th Infantry Division of Patton's Third Army it becomes a matter of life or death for an endless week. Facing them is an SS regiment willing to fight them to the death. How long is this supposed to last? What day is it? Or has time stopped? This is no way to live anymore.

"Hi Wisconsin, we've got another one here." A dead German, a fallen soldier who looks like he's peacefully sleeping against a steel beam. His helmet is tipped toward the back of his head, his hand on his chin, making it look as if he wants to tell the whole world something.

They succeed in taking 1,500 SS prisoners. "Arms up!" If they don't see from the uniform or the skull on their cap that a soldier is a member of the SS, they can see it from the blood type mark on the underarm. Should they wear a thin woolen shirt, then the Patton boys know for sure: this is a scoundrel. In that case the 'noblemen' have to lie flat on the ground for a day and a night. "Cut them down to size," that's what the General ordered. Should one raise his head after a day, then in the most favorable case a bullet comes whistling close to his head followed by another day of flat on the belly. For Patton, members of the SS may be transported as POWs, but with their heads bowed.

Later on Nanno with his 90th Division unit is closed-in for six weeks, while farther on they're grievously needed and awaited. Before, behind, and on both flanks the immovable German fortifications keep them under fire. Where are the paratroopers now when they are needed? Where are the English bombers to do the rough preparatory work? It is a terrible time. Finally they come, the Tommies with their heavy B-17s. Two thousand allied bombers fly in and out, heavy with bombs coming in and empty going out.

"And now after them." Caterpillar truck driver Nanno Hiemstra advances too, even if they're still not farther than Normandy.

An ear-shattering blow. The Cat's blown off the road and gets stuck between two tree trunks. Left and right, grenades knock splinters off the trees. He wrestles himself from behind the wheel, lets himself drop down from the Cat, and then it's quiet. Dead still. Or do his ears fail him again? The moment that he realizes he's still alive, chauffeur Richie appears from the Cat behind him.

"Hi Wisconsin, how are you doing?"

"Could be worse." He's standing again, and he remembers that he's got an ax hanging on the truck. Both trees have to come down. One hour later the Cat rolls again, two hours later they're back in contact with the convoy. That night there's no chance for an hour of sleep; at the edge of a forest they have to let the howitzers clamor.

The day arrives when large units of the Third Army run out of fuel. Patton in tough language demands from Commander Eisenhower fuel for all his materiel. "When there's no longer food for my men, they'll eat their boots, but don't think that they can pee gasoline!"

The German air attacks continue and 'Wisconsin' cannot advance with his Caterpillar and all that hangs behind. Finally, there's gas again. Now go. Again he's one of the fragile links in an endless column, which at night with extinguished lights over winding roads try to gain some terrain. And then it's stop, and more blasts. And hits, of course. After a link in the convoy has been shot to scrap and Red Cross trucks with death loaded in the back race up and down,

123

they have to regroup. Keep going. Stop! Try going through open fields then. No, no chance, a truck flies up into the air, it's littered with landmines.

It is the evening of July 30, the sky is clear but there's thunder around the city of Avranches. Nanno sits with a steaming mug of coffee, staring ahead, when an officer appears who's looking for him.

"Soldier Nanno Hiemstra?"

"Yes sir!" He's told that in the coming night he will drive at the head of the column into the city of Avranches. "Because we want to have that city in our hands by tomorrow night! You have to thoroughly orient yourself, you will be at the head and will lead the materiel first to and then through the city center of Avranches. You will take position on the northeast side of the square, and from that point, with the infantry of the 90th, you will mow down those damn Germans. Everybody at the same time, and otherwise one by one. And when you're finished, you have to drive farther northeast, with the troops behind you."

The subordinate from Wisconsin wants to say something too; he says that he's just become a dad, and that… but the officer is not ready to tell his story again.

Avranches is burning, but that's not the worst: the resistance is so all-out powerful. Snipers, machine gun and grenade fire. With his steel brother-in-arms he searches for the path that he's imprinted on his brain by studying the city map. There's no time to look around now; it's as if he's the only one riding into the city. Whole blocks of homes that have been erased confuse his sense of direction; it becomes a gamble. Here and there he sees personnel from his 90th Division who are there to give his column cover.

All around him there's flaming firepower, but he succeeds in reaching the city center. With the Cat hiding between two walls of a skeleton that once was a church, he looks around. His column! Without too many links missing. Now he will need to be the first to hurry to the center square, and then across it, but which street must he take to reach the northeast side of the city? The enemy is smart enough to turn the signposts to point in the wrong direction.

Then something happens that he will never forget: someone is running as hard as he can across the square with a white flag right toward his Caterpillar. Is it the guide who's been designated by the French resistance to show the Americans the way? One wouldn't think so, because it turns out to be a boy of somewhere around sixteen.

"That way, sir!" Nanno sees a burning city in a pair of dark eyes. But does he also see the truth in those eyes?

"That way," the boy repeats, and he points to a narrow street that exits on the other end of the square. Why shouldn't it be the other, wider street? Nanno hesitates. Right behind him a grenade explodes; here life is short-lived.

"Say boy, point me the way to the northeast! Now!" Nanno grabs the boy by his chin. Two big eyes. Tears. Whistling bullets, but the boy doesn't duck; crying from the stress and agitation he points again emphatically to the narrowest passage.

"Yes, boy?"

"Oui, mon libérateur." Nanno signals the column behind him, accelerates, hears an explosion right behind him, looks around for the boy – what happened to the boy? For the first time since Utah Beach, Nanno again hollers aloud while he races across the square like a madman: "This boy must go home again!"

Years later he will relive this scene in scary dreams, still always calling out loudly as he chases across the square of Avranches: "This boy must go home again." Because that boy showed him the right way.

Nanno survived the summer of blood, sweat and tears – just the summer. After heavy fighting, they make their way across the Mayenne River, they win the battle for the Seine, and they can taste for a few days the sweet life of a liberated city full of the liberated. But they know they need to keep going after the enemy. The Germans, fighting all the way, have let themselves be pushed back into the Heimat, but they're of no mind to surrender. They've dug themselves in massively in the Ardennes and have seen a chance to fortify their positions on the east side of the Mosel and Saar. Now that the winter of 1944-45 is underway, more heavy sacrifices await the 90th Division of Patton's Army.

A dark night in the Ardennes. A wet snow shower, fog and glazed frost. It's impossible to scale the steep elevations. Repeatedly the Germans, hidden in camouflaged machine gun nests, end the lives of another buddy or two.

Nanno's Cat waits somewhere behind the front in a camouflaged shed. As an infantryman he must now try to survive in a foxhole he dug himself. It's his fourth night in frozen earth. Where were they a few days ago? Oh yes, in a barn full of hungry animals. Do they have the enemy in a trap here in the high hills, or have they themselves run into a trap? When the Germans make no sound, watch out. Till General Patton has had enough and orders his men to go after the enemy. Each soldier gets orders to pray en masse for victory, at a time set in advance.

For 41 days Nanno has not undressed. The general decrees that they cannot have their breakfast and warm coffee until they have turned in their pair of wet and dirty socks. "Because a frontline soldier with untended and open sores on his feet is walking on his last leg."

One afternoon, Nanno and his buddies locate four machine gun nests. Who, at 60 yards, can accurately aim a hand grenade? "New Jersey!" Now that snow is on the ground, frontline soldiers have white overalls and white painted guns. "Let's go, buddy, they won't see us come."

The way one can hardly stand oneself without a change of clothes for weeks, the same way one's spirit can also become grimy. How

126

long has it been since he thought about the dearest in his life? How's it possible that for a whole day he hasn't given a thought to his lovely wife and tender baby? It seems like a mere instinct has taken the place of human feelings. Survive, it doesn't matter how.

On a stone-cold February morning Nanno observes in bewilderment a beautiful sunrise. As if he had no longer expected this miracle. He sits in his Cat again, rides in convoy along winding asphalt strewn with dead bodies. Mostly German. "Damn," stammers 'New Jersey' beside him, "dead we are all the same."

At long last his division has arrived at the Mosel, but no matter where they try to cross, they land within easy range of an SS regiment that has dug itself into the hills on the other side of the river. From that position they can mow away with their accurate artillery and heavy machine guns. It is Nanno's role to be in the lead again for crossing the river. Not only for the 80,000 men that are left of the division, but especially also for the tanks, pieces of artillery, and trucks.

When they're halfway through building a pontoon bridge, all hell breaks loose from the other side of the river. Even if the bridge were finished, no one would cross to the other side alive.

Again they lay a bridge, now a few hundred yards downstream and hopefully beyond the enemy's range. At the same time it gives their own troops more cover.

Four of a group of fifteen Caterpillar drivers receive the command to risk it, and Nanno is one of the four. They have to give it a try, across the pontoon bridge pulled askew by the stream and half sunk. He succeeds in making it alive through the barrage of fire with some men and weapons. Having arrived on the other side, out of breath and soaked, he has to turn right around and go back with four casualties and twelve wounded. They lie in front of him, behind him, at times tight against him. And when he has delivered them, he has to go through that hell again, now with a praying

127

chaplain beside him. Once again back across the river, with the silent dead, the screaming wounded, and a chaplain with the Bible in one hand and a hand in the other.

It is as if someone is standing by Nanno as he crosses the Mosel three times in a row; he is never hit. The last crossing turns out to be the least risky; on the east side of the Mosel the cannons, the howitzers and machine guns fall silent. His new relief driver alerts him to the fact that it is Sunday morning. On the west side of the river the sun is shining, on the east side there's still a morning haze. Farther on where the river bends, at the foot of a hill, he sees a town. White houses with damaged roofs in blue and red, here and there a plume of smoke. The top of a church spire hangs crooked.

The next morning they advance farther into Germany. Here and there the smoldering remains testify of a fierce battle. The rumor is that the Wehrmacht will now with might and main try to keep the Americans from crossing the Rhine.

With steel tracks under the Cat Nanno rumbles on along broken roads and through open fields. Here a lifeless town, there a city bombed into ruins. In the last week of March 1945 he realizes that it's been a year since he boarded the Ethicon Castle. He must've sailed below Iceland when his daughter was born. Now and then he rereads the telegram that reached him two days before Avranches. A baby girl, so healthy, so beautiful. Lorraine, a name with a ring of freedom. He tries to call up the image of that dear innocence, but it is the glance of the mother that takes over, her full breasts; a rush of desire courses through his body, the way rushes of fear have also done.

They still have to fight their way across the Rhine. Who's going to survive? Who isn't? Nanno thinks of the first sentence in his dad's first letter, which he first read somewhere in the Ardennes: "It's good growing weather here, but Nanno my boy, Mom and I think about you more often than about the weather."

128

A few days later he thunders behind the columns of Sherman tanks right across sprouting patches of meadows and farmland where the unreaped harvest of last fall lies in decay. At the edge of the town they take time for a break. Some half-dozen men find a comfortable spot in a gully to catch some rays of the spring sun. They offer each other a cigarette.

"Buddy, give me a light!"

"You have time for two cigarettes, that's all!"

Nanno takes his stengun, strolls over the farmyard, and feels the heat of the sun when he touches the shed's brick wall. Farther on a dead horse blocks the stable door. On the patch of lawn in front of the farmhouse deep-blue crocuses stick their head above the new grass. He's about to go around the corner to return to his buddies when he comes face to face with a woman. She must be the farmer's wife. The woman doesn't show a sign of surprise. He's enjoying this encounter and reaches out his hand, but she beats him to it, she grabs his hand and walks alongside him. But then, while still holding his hand, she turns to him, and what he sees is a mother. She's all in black, like his mom in the three months after Grandma Ytsje's death. She's in mourning. He stands beside her and can see over her, the way he could see over his own mom on the small train station platform in Sharon. He takes off his helmet.

"Handsome young man," she says, "I've lost everything!" She points to her house, her field with grape vines that have been plowed under by the tanks, and makes clear to him that that isn't the worst. "The scars in the field will fade in time, but the scars of a mother who first lost her husband and then two of her sons will never heal!"

Is it possible that all mothers have one and the same voice?

"Come on, Wisconsin!" One of his buddies calls out. "We still have to cross that stupid little ditch of the Rhine. And then we go to Berlin and grab Hitler by the balls."

At Oppenheim he has to cross the Rhine with the 90th. The Rhine could not possibly be worse than the Mosel, could it? Worry and tension return. Or is it total fear? They wait till dark. Then the foreboding picture of three of his buddies who risk going across in a small boat to check things out. When they're back at last, they have useful information. Not there, but a little farther on the pontoon bridge must be laid.

Across! The Germans still prove to have heavily armed Fock-Wulf fighter planes; some of them will not reach the other side alive. When it is soldier Nanno's turn, thirty feet in front of him a GMC truck full of gasoline is hit and goes up in flames. "Thank you, focking-Wulf, for giving us some light."

Nanno's new relief driver is a busy talker, but truck driver Wisconsin, never much of a talker anyway, has been mostly silenced by the war.

The Main River. Frankfurt, city of fear. Snipers, hidden in carcasses of stone, defend a city that has no heart and soul. Right behind him, two dull thwacks, as if a tablecloth is shaken out. When he turns around, he sees a buddy crumple right in front of him. And at the Mosel he had been spared.

Beginning of April 1945. Nanno is there when the 90th Infantry Division liberates concentration camp Flossenbürg, not far from the Czech border. Not till decades later does he decide to tell about it. He wouldn't have, except that one of his large number of grandchildren asks him about it. And that boy is the spitting image of the boy in Avranches. "I want to know, Grandpa, I want to hear it from Grandpa himself," the boy says. And then he tells, he passes it on, but then the unbearable images reappear, of the boy, of the emaciated souls who stared at him through large eyes in hollow eye sockets. "They no longer had hope or tears, and now they had to cry from joy."

Of the 90,000 inmates in Flossenbürg, 30,000 had died by the day of liberation.

Now it is May 8, for time does not seem to be able to stand still. Germany capitulates. Exhausted and battered, a large part of the 90th Infantry Division of the 3rd American Army is camped in and around the town of Bodenwöhr. Thousands of military, endless columns of heavy equipment, temporary barracks and kitchens and hospitals. There Nanno says farewell to his brother-in-arms of iron and steel, his Cat. "No, not a single emotion over the scars in the steel." Or are there? Tall Corporal Hiemstra needs to be alone for a moment. He strolls through the village, sees a mother with a small girl standing in an open front door and asks how old the girl is. She turns out to be a little over a year old. "My girl is the same age, but I've never seen her."

Low in the east the elevations of Bohemia rise against a purple evening sky. A twisted place-name sign full of bullet holes dangles on its side as the first war monument of the Second World War. Whisky is exchanged for vodka, in the distance an accordion is playing, and a number of Russian soldiers are dancing the Cossack dance. He sees vagrants loiter about timidly in shabby clothing; they are forced laborers and other displaced persons from every nook and cranny of Europe. Most of them nearly worked themselves to death in the Messerschmitt factories on the other side of town.

"Where is east, sir? I have to go east." And: "Will you give me something to eat?" They don't know if their family survived the war, if their house is still there. They see the Americans as their saviors.

The next morning there are two letters from Alice, two envelopes full of longing. Yes, it's going well with our girl. "Daddy, come home." He has to answer that perhaps he will have to stay till September to help arrange the transport of the army materiel to Antwerp. The Americans after all are still at war, even though that's playing out only in the Far East. "And of course greetings from your parents. Dad David is so glad that the war is over; if you have time and a chance, Nanno, pay a visit to Friesland, to the town with the

stubby tower that your grandma told you so many stories about."
But as it turns out, for Nanno there is only one town: Sharon, Wisconsin, where love and the future are waiting.

FLIGHT

The same war, but then a few years earlier. Meindert Boorsma finds himself with his combat buddies seven miles from Zagreb. The Croatian winter is harsh, and the enemy is too, but one day there's good news: "All is well. Croatia has fallen." Still that same day another message follows: "And now on to the Volga! Stalingrad!" The communication strikes him as hard and bitter cold. He entertains the thought again of vanishing into thin air, but where would he go? Flee from under the flag? He sees himself running away as hard as he can and then smashing forward to the ground with a load of lead in his back. "Auf der Flucht erschossen." [Shot in flight.] His most trusted comrade Wolfgang Hanssen would like to escape too, but what did Wolfie whisper a few days ago? "Meinhart, there's no getting away anymore, we have to try to survive."

Can it possibly become more vicious than against the partisans? For three days and nights they had their hands full with the partisans. Of his commando group of eighteen they lost five. The thirteen of them were surrounded, their only chance for survival lay in their being better shots and quicker than the partisans. He lay behind a heavy tree trunk, waiting for his chance, and suddenly he heard admonitions from his childhood. His dad's voice, the same words as when he was ready for his first school ice skating race on the Dolte in Workum: "Watch it, Meindert, be first, don't let anybody screw you, you can beat him!"

Two days and nights they had gone without food, and they even made it through the barrage of hand grenades. But all right, there was still some ammunition for a couple of machine guns. Rickatickatickatick...

"All clear!" Meindert and Wolfgang Hanssen don't trust it, there must be some partisans still around.

Winter goes on and on, there's a big layer of snow. You can't find nicer Christmas cards to send than with this winter scene. It's quiet in the forest. Dead quiet. The trimmed trees rise frozen toward the sky. One more night he digs himself in with his commando group; the last partisan can still cause hell on earth. The next morning everything is truly clear, they can try to join one of the SS commando groups on the other side of town on the hill farther on. For the umpteenth time he digs a hole, not only in the snow, but deeper, in the frozen earth.

"Come, Meinhart, deeper."

"The others are already done."

"A handbreadth deeper, then you're safe."

When it's so quiet and freezing fifteen degrees, any sound carries far. While one of his buddies stands guard, he settles down deep into the ground on a small stack of slender branches and some brush.

"A bird catcher must think himself warm." While he's on the way to a few winks, he hears his dad saying it. His ears still buzz from yesterday's hand grenades. He thinks himself warm, imagines himself behind the hiding place deep in the Heidenskip Common, hears the rustling of the reeds and the panting of the waves against the basalt. And thus he sinks further and further into sleep.

But then it happens, then it's like the whole earth is exploding and he's lifted out of his grave. He falls down again, along with a load of snow with something warm to cover him, tries to get his breath, doesn't know if he's dead or alive.

"Don't let anybody screw you!" He remains motionless. The partisans have come, with hand grenades.

A while later. Above him and to the side he hears moaning, the cursing of his own people, the voice of Wolfie Hanssen, "Meinhart!"

"All clear." He risks climbing to the surface, and there things look terrible. Blood, snow, and mud. Three hand grenades delivered three dead enemies to the partisans. And now ten of them are left. Footsteps in the snow show his squad their heels. The footprints indicate only three partisans.

"Where is Ernst Lohmann, our sentry?" Is that his bloody shoe? No, Lohmann stood guard farther on. "Where are the footprints of Lohmann!" Worst case he's been taken as a bonus by the partisans. "If so, he would've been better off if he'd been killed immediately."

"How could Ernst let himself get screwed like that."

"We're going to get Lohmann back!" Meindert has never seen Squad Leader Lübke so furious. "The skunks must've come from the hamlet on the other side of the woods. Look, their footprints. Find them and finish them off in their own stinking nest!" Lübke selects three men to carry out the assignment: the radio operator, Eckhart Koch, Wolfie Hanssen, "and you, Meinhart." Of course, it didn't escape the Squad Leader that Eckhart, Wolfie, and he are close buddies.

They're leaving well-armed: one light machine gun, two regular guns with bayonet, each a revolver, and the last three hand grenades of the squad.

Eckhart takes the chance to ask for some food along. "Nein! You had your ration this afternoon. If you're not back tomorrow morning before four o'clock, that will have been your last meal. Tomorrow there will be some more to eat for lunch."

They get fifteen minutes to study the ordnance map, don a white camouflage overall, and follow the footprints of the Croats. It's as if the woods are still whizzing from the recent violence. "We're in luck," Wolfie whispers. "The sky is clouding over, visibility is getting worse." It was indeed only three men who walked back at a steady pace. Not a single imprint from Ernst Lohmann's boots. It doesn't even appear that they dragged him along. Of course, they surprised Ernst from behind. Lohmann, with the sound of silence in his head, deafened by the explosion and the fear. Of course, they threw a snare over his helmet, made of steel wire, and strangled him. And then, without leaving a trace of blood, buried him in the snow.

Meindert tries hard to control his rising fear. Not together through the forest, but apart from each other, from tree to tree. The footprints lead the threesome to an open field. Ahead, against the hills, must be the village of the partisans; the map says that it's not much more than twenty houses. Not a light anywhere. "But they must be there!" Eckhart proposes not to follow the footprints any longer but to walk around the village in a wide circle. "Into the village from the other side, where they don't expect us." It's starting to snow, heavily. Now and then they can barely see, but the snow keeps it from getting dark.

An hour and a half later they stand on the other side of the village behind a wooden cattle shed. A humble farmhouse sits tight against it. Had they seen a dim light a moment ago, or not? Had they heard some male voices? They decide to wait fifteen minutes, without moving a muscle. When the fifteen minutes are up, they still wait, motionless. It's getting even quieter around the place. There's a soft whisper: "They must be here."

"Why don't they have someone on guard, then?"

"They think they killed all of us."

In the meantime it has been snowing so hard that their own footprints are no longer visible.

"You or I?" Gestures Wolfie.

All fear ebbs away from Meindert; he appoints himself. Is it because of the cow barn smell that is so familiar to him? If there are no partisans here, then there must be some food to be rustled up.

The barn doors are locked, as in every war. "Give me our last hand grenades!" He gestures.

He smells cattle, hears the animals sniff and rumble. On the side of the old shed he finds a couple of loose boards in the wall. Every time a cow snorts or coughs, he wiggles a board loose with the bayonet. He succeeds in quietly sneaking his way inside the shed. He's landed in pitch darkness. The cattle react nervously, but soon everything is back to normal. No, don't turn on his flashlight yet, first get used to the dark. The animals run loose, it must be a kind of deep litter barn. Wait a minute, here's something like a gate, a partition. In the meanwhile it turns out not to be pitch dark at all; on the other side of the gate it looks like there's a thick layer of clean straw on the floor; where the cattle will be moved later.

Suddenly he gets a terrible craving for fresh milk and searches for the udder of a milk cow. After a couple of mistakes, he succeeds and milks himself in the mouth. Now he has to risk turning on his flashlight. He does it while holding the light deep inside his pocket. He's got just enough light this way.

With the revolver in his hand and a hand grenade within quick reach, he takes a chance on getting past the straw to a door and stands in the only living space of the little farm. Will he be able – if he has the hand grenades ready to pull the safety ring and throw – to get to the opening in the wooden wall of the shed? Yes, he should be able to.

In the cramped room he notices a small table and a couple of chairs. The inside blinds are closed, the stove is still warm enough to warm his hands on it. An oil lamp on the wall. Damn, it feels lukewarm, there sure as hell must be someone living here. He risks taking the lit flashlight from his pocket. Light. And at the same moment he sees that a door in the wall is slowly opening. With the finger on the trigger he's ready to waste a Croatian. He rams the door farther open and stands face to face with an old man who tries to get out from under a load of blankets. A very old man with a silver-gray beard and a fearless glance.

"Partisans, where partisans?" Meindert wants to know.

The man shakes his old head and sits down. Eyes too old to show fear. Meindert clears out the pile of blankets and starts searching for weapons. There's nothing. He more or less throws the covers over the little man again. Why, as hungry as he is, is he too timid to demand some food from this old fellow who's on his last legs?

With the flashlight he trudges between the skinny cows to the loose boards in the shed's wall. Then he turns around one more time and shines the flashlight around the deep litter space. What?

Is that a hatch carefully lifted up in the straw and then immediately lowered again? He gives it no second thought, lunges toward it with two hand grenades ready to toss, lifts the hatch a few inches, flings the whole load of deathly horror inside, races to the opening in the wall, and gets stuck. What happens after that he does not experience fully consciously, but he's blown through the hole by a tremendous blast.

"All's well," they're able to report to the Squad Leader when they return. "All cleared up."

"That was advisable, because Carstens, Baring, and Alker are dead." "And sentry Ernst Lohmann?" "He's dead too, he lay not far from the sleep holes under the snow. Only his head was missing." Squad leader Lübke: "We put him in one of the holes, we're not taking the body with us. One who lets himself be screwed by such fiends is not worth a grave."

In the course of the next day the nine of them are able to join depleted commando group 315. Finally there's something to eat again. The men give each other just brief reports of their actions, the consequences weigh on them heavily enough. That afternoon they witness one of those consequences: in the square in the middle of the village with the wooden cow shed the very last of the partisans early that morning hanged the little old man with the silver-gray beard by his heels from a pole for suspected treason.

After Stalingrad they're done; the German Sixth Army under General Friedrich Paulus has surrendered to the Russians. But the men don't get to know about that last part; they only know that they have to be some fifteen hundred miles north. On to Leningrad. "And when we have our claws on that city, Moscow will be a cinch." After four months they know better. It's mid-April. Meindert finds himself in a fortification not far from the Gulf of Finland, deep in his pocket a letter and a keepsake from Dad and Mom. A letter, decorated on its long bureaucratic journey with Reich- and SS-stamps.

[...] You're all the way in Russia now, Meindert. Did you see the Plovers there? Come back from the South? They have their Homeland high up in the Northeast. Did you get the warm Winter Clothes we sent you? Then you must also have found the Plover Whistle, it is the same as the one we had with us in the Heidenskip Commons, you remember. Mother and I wanted you to have that. [...]

The steady handwriting of Dad, with the greetings from a trembling mother's hand. He has read the letter only once; he's reluctant to do it again. Why? He has no idea. But of one thing he's certain: should the hour come that he has to surrender to the Russians, he will hold this letter above his head with both hands and call out "Hollanski, Hollanski." He will try to explain to them that he doesn't belong in this war, he will show them the bone whistle that he's worn night and day on a string underneath his thin woolen undershirt.

It's winter again. They have as good as surrounded Leningrad – the old St. Petersburg – for a couple of months already and bombarded it with hundreds of thousands grenades, and yet a group of citizens succeed in escaping the city. There they go, with their carts and sleds. A defenseless line of wretches. Dark dots against a snow-white décor. Wrestling through the whirling snow with bent backs and struggling across frozen streams and rivers, across a snow-covered lake with here and there a steaming dark hole – he sees them in the far distance stumble over the eternally untrustworthy Luga River.

"Quit shooting, Eckhart, they have children with them. Look, they're going down to damnation. Dear God, they're drowning in front of our eyes!"

"That's why I'm shooting. To die from one shot is better than gradually starve to death."

How long is this madness still bearable? Is it better to shoot himself in the head like that animal, Squad Leader Lübke, did? Should he, against all logic, survive this hell, then the things he has seen will haunt him for the rest of his life.

It has been the winter of meaninglessness, and yet it becomes spring again. And summer. The cannons continue to bark, and that has awakened a horrendously cruel beast. And it's coming: the Red Army. Above the eastern horizon the rumble begins. With might and main the positions of the Wehrmacht have to be fortified. Is Eckhart right and are the hordes now coming by the millions across the Urals to get them?

On the longest day the men of Fortification 216 get a couple of hours off to stretch their legs. Meindert no longer indulges in the illusion of escape. He tramps through a village where at the most only a cat might still be alive. A little while ago he was still hanging out with his small group of brothers-in-arms, but now he finds himself alone. He steps inside a small green house through an open door, sees himself in a high narrow mirror. He's shocked; is that him? He asks the man in the mirror who he is. No answer. The man in the mirror can't let it go, undresses himself completely to check whether it's really him; he sees that what's left of him is as skinny as a beanpole. He must already have lost his soul. Yes, a plover whistle on a string still dangles around his skinny neck. He raises both of his bony arms and shows the SS mark in his left arm pit, and he knows now that his old name doesn't fit him anymore; he will live on as a man without a soul. How much longer?

"Mom, I promise Mom that I will come home again." He doesn't even have his own voice anymore. Completely defeated, he gets dressed and rejoins the other men. They're pretty excited that Meinhart is back because the cannon flesh of the Wehrmacht has been thinning out considerably. "Keep in mind that we can't expect any more reinforcements. Each one has to fight for two." And someone else adds: "We make up the last portion of Heil Hitler."

It becomes fall 1944. The days are getting shorter, and once again

140

there are two traincars with frontline prostitutes. Today it's Group North's turn to be rewarded for services rendered. Numb and without inclination he's resting on the woman's body. His wonderment and desire turn into helplessness and self-pity. The woman – no longer young – says that she understands. A moment without words and gratification. Only a crumb of comfort.

In the southeast the boom-boom steadily thunders louder, more massive, more threatening, till the sky and the ground tremble. At first they smell the smoke from the scorched steppes on the stiff winter wind from the southeast, now it comes roaring their way. They come to take revenge and are thereby accompanied by the winter cold of 1944-45. A cold more deadly than the two thousand cannons and three thousand tanks of the Red Army. Meindert sees footsteps in the snow that run dead in a white endlessness, and a frozen hand sticking out of the snow as a grotesque symbol of the madness.

And he, only son of Johannes and Pytsje from the houseboat, is one of the hundreds of thousands who had let themselves get dragged along, or who simply were swept up in it. Three hundred and seventy days he had camped out in desperate conditions before old St. Petersburg; more than a hundred thousand bombs and grenades they had disgorged over a city with three million poor souls. At the end of the madness some seven hundred thousand starving poor wretches will be left. Hitler may regard them as subhuman creatures, but whoever can still fight keeps fighting fearlessly for wife and children. Behind them they know of the comrades of the advancing Red Army. Now far past the Urals they're advancing in a front a thousand miles wide. With four times as many men, cannons, tanks, airplanes, icebreakers, and war ships than the Germans have in 1944 on the eastern and western fronts. And do they know inside the fortifications before Leningrad that the Americans have already reached the Rhine? No, they don't know that.

It happens in a period of dry, mild, even pleasant winter weather.

On an afternoon, their gun platforms fall silent, and in response the boom-boom from the other side also appears to quieten down. That silence... It's as if they used the roar of the cannons only to cover up their fear.

For a moment they can raise their heads above the ground without fear of losing them. And what do they see? There's still earth, still land, but not a landscape. No flower that blooms, not a bird that sings. This place will show up on a map, but its life has been shot out of it. Should a Creator exist, then He would now call out: "Look around you and ask yourself what kind of land you've been fighting for!"

Meindert's brother-in-arms Wolfgang Hanssen was spared this shattered, broken picture. Already a year ago Wolfie had confided that he'd give his right hand to escape this hell. Shortly after that he did it, raised one hand above the trench, and right after that he had only one hand left. Wolfie landed in the hospital ward, but not for long – five weeks later he was already put on guard duty. Instead of going home, merely guard duty. At first he was in luck, because they couldn't prove that he had done it on purpose. But he was betrayed, placed against a wall in front of the whole squad, and shot dead.

Beginning of 1945. They have to pull back farther but want to build new fortifications. Meindert does not realize that the urge for survival has faded into apathy. For how can it be that he's sitting here half asleep against a wooden fence? Oh, but he's in his hiding place again, intent on catching golden plovers, in the back part of Hanke Noordeloos's field on the edge of Sand Lake in the Heidenskip, longing for that one song that speaks of hope. Where is that one short touch of the bow on the taut strings, that one sign of life from her who loved him?

But again and again it's the racket of the grenades that banishes his hope.

One evening there's a Schnapps for everyone. And another. With strong gin they try to dismiss the madness from their minds. His rail-thin body already dozes after less than two drinks, his weariness is indeed doused with some hope, with desire for her again. He hears himself call her name, "Jetske." Dear girl, I didn't choose this, you should now be able to judge me, but not then. All I wanted was to be free and happy with you. Don't abandon me, weren't we created for each other? Look me straight in the eyes one more time, give me your lips once more, let me taste you! In a drunken dream he dances with her down their secret path that runs through Jonkershuzen, Dedzjum, and Parregea to Hieslum, and from there turns on Tempel Road to the Nijhuzum coast. There he sees Dad and Mom stand in front of their houseboat. From a distance they wave to him and his good-looking girlfriend. "Here I come with my love," he calls out to them. But then it turns out that it's only his fate he has with him, and he calls: "Mom, I'm here, I your little boy, I'm here."

But all this will change; in the trench they will soon receive their first Russian visitor. It happens when he, together with the machine-gunner Peter Tahlhammer, hunkers in a deep mud hole, not far from an anti-tank ditch, and hear enemy fire come closer and closer. There he is then. Ivan.

High above them, on the edge of the tank ditch, he appears, stumbles, raises his hands, drops his gun, makes a half turn and smacks down close to them on the hard clods.

Peter stands ready with his bayonet, Meindert shouts "he's already dead." The Russian's legs below the knees are mostly gone, his crotch is darkening with blood, half unconscious the Russian turns his head to them. They see the face of a boy who's never yet shaved; it's as if he wants to say something to them. It takes a moment before they realize that he's asking for the coup de grace; with his right index finger he gestures a trigger pull.

"Peter, let him do it himself, give him your revolver."

"Then he's going to shoot us first."

Tahlhammer never takes long to decide, Meindert can hardly

turn his face away in time. "Bang!"

"Your birthday present," quips Tahlhammer later in the day. It is February 25, 1945; today Meindert Boorsma turns 26. "Quite an age for a soldier on the eastern front," Tahlhammer comments. "Hearty congratulations."

Not so much later there's the call, it sounds like for the last time, "Zurück!" "Retreat, on the double!" Who manages to jump on the back of a combat vehicle? Leningrad is abandoned, the men of his squadron wander away from their command. Chaos. 'We' now changes into 'I,' and 'I' want to survive. Behind him some of his comrades seem to be taken war prisoners; there are stories that they can choose between having their throat slit or Siberia.

Meindert has little sense of time anymore, walks in the uniform of a regular Wehrmacht infantry soldier. Except for the SS sign in his armpit, he doesn't have a single mark or paper on him anymore. Only the plover whistle still dangles on his bony chest. Underneath his stolen long military coat a stolen chunk of sour bread and some cold coffee in a metal field bottle.

A few days later on a late afternoon, Meindert follows railroad tracks running in a southwesterly direction. He hides in the bushes when for the third time a Wehrmacht train approaches. When it's become dark and a fourth one approaches, he grabs his chance when the train has almost come to a standstill. It pulls ahead and then stops anew. It turns out to be a passenger train instead of a freight train, and seemingly hardly armed. He's able to jump on the footboard, but he can't open the entry door. The train starts moving again, he sees a deep bank in front of him, can no longer jump off safely, but then the caravan stops again. He takes the chance to crawl to the other side of the wagon under the steel connectors between two train units.

Right in front of him he sees the boots of a soldier who with his back toward him is taking a leak. He hops on the footboard, darts through the open door, and is in the train. In the dim light of the inside he sees wounded and apparently dead bodies lie on the floor;

144

a nurse or helper hardly pays attention to him as he moves to another wagon. Unnoticed, he lies down, between the living and the dead. Huffing and puffing, the train is back in motion.

Later in the night a Red Cross soldier comes who wants to know "if I can do something here."

"We don't have much more to offer here than a little comfort," he answers, "and not even that."

"I know. There's no blood left, there are hardly medicines on this shitty train; all I know is that they're up to wagon 17 with the morphine."

"Good. Morphine."

A crippled petty officer passes, not so young anymore, who asks under which section he served. He manages to convince the man that he was sent on the train as nurse by Captain Werner Poth of the infantry company, position 115. He used to hear Wolfie brag about the recently fallen Captain Poth. He finds out that the train has seventeen wagons, with the three at the end reserved for the dead. "As long as it's freezing, we're taking them along," says the crippled petty officer. "In another day and a half we've hopefully reached the Polish border."

By fits and starts they rumble day in and day out toward the west. Each day there's just enough to eat and drink to stay alive. Meindert manages to lay his hands on some medicine for his skin rash and anemia.

In Poland they are attacked twice, but it turns out all right. From remarks by the crippled Red Cross man he finds out that in the city, where they stopped for half a night to load up one thing or another, they were not only shot at but also shat upon. "A group of men and women stood on a viaduct and peed and shat on our back two wagons. So great is the hate that they dirtied even our dead and seriously wounded."

An eternity later, the final stop. The train appears to have made the Oder. Meindert Boorsma gathers from the conversations that they have indeed reached the vicinity of Frankfurt on the Oder.

"They blew up the bridge to keep the Russians back."

"We have to cross, but can't now."

The train is at a silent standstill; in the east the roar and thunder of war continues. In the train depot a coal shack has to be turned into an emergency hospital. Would he be able to escape here? Yes, but where to? How wide is the Oder? What's left of that railway bridge? He'd better first help get the wounded inside the building.

When it's nearly night, he hears a surgeon say to his assistant: "The barbarians from the east have never heard of the Red Cross."

Meindert begins to prepare for his escape, manages to gather some extra food and liquids, and offers to substitute for the ailing guard. In the night, close to three, when the coast seems clear, he stands before the river with a backpack made from sturdy sailcloth and containing Red Cross clothes and some provisions. He can see the destroyed railway bridge up ahead a ways. The weather could've been worse; the moon is dark but it's not exactly pitch-dark. Cold but no wind. The river looks to be the narrowest by the destroyed railway bridge, but crossing is going to be more than a hundred yards. Here and there pieces of wreckage stick out; there are a couple of places where the bridge is almost totally gone.

His war of attrition begins on a piece of bridge wreckage that sticks halfway out of the river. He scrambles from beam to beam, from pillar to pillar. Twice he has to dip to his waist into the ice-cold and flowing water, but then he can reach the next twisted pillar along a stretched-out, loose-hanging wire. Seized by the cold, he yet continues onto another piece of broken steel. But at a given moment he can't go on. His last ounce of strength is depleted, he's even too tired to cry. Not far away he sees the river bank. Take a deep breath, then push on. But it doesn't work; will he be torn along by the current and drown after all? He nearly has hold of another steel beam, but his backpack hooks onto a piece of iron just below the water surface. The will not to give up has not quite left him, not for the whole long crossing; he makes it.

The Oder, that magical boundary, he's on the other side. Weeping with pain, cold, and exhaustion, lying down he tries to take off his wet clothes. When he finally succeeds, he slings the wet bundle in the river and claws the clothes with the Red Cross labels from his backpack. They didn't quite stay dry and are therefore hard to get on. When he's finally dressed, his whole body is shaking. It takes a supreme effort to move one leg in front of the other.

Much later he arrives at a farm which at the break of day he already had in view. It looks like its residents left hearth and home in a hurry; all the doors are open, the cattle are gone. Yes, in the abandoned horse stable there's a pile of manure that's no more than two days old. The farmer took off with all his stuff with horse and wagon.

First he has to try to dry his feet. He stumbles onto a pair of work shoes that fit him pretty well. Darn, in the front part of the place there are a couple of piles of clothes in one of the cabinets, without a doubt from the farmer himself: underpants with patches for the knees, neat blue outer pants, a heavy farmer's jacket. When he's put them on and feels the comfort, he can't help crying. Wait, the cord with the plover whistle came off over his head. Here, you! The whistle has to go back to the houseboat. If it is not his comfort bird, then it's his guardian angel.

In the cellar he finds some food and drink that's passable, takes off for the barn, makes himself a nest in the hay, and goes to sleep.

After at least twelve hours he wakes soaked with sweat. No matter how much he tries, he can't get to his feet. Fever? With painful abrasions on his whole body, he dozes off again. It must've been another hour or so when he wakes up again, this time by heavy thumping in the east. It won't be long anymore till the Russians reach the Oder.

The weather has greatly improved, it's almost spring-like now. For the second time he takes the stairs to the loft of the house to inspect the surroundings through the dormer window. His only view is to the southwest. He spots a narrow road that runs dead into the horizon. Soon he will take that direction.

Everything here tells him that a man pottered about all by himself. The single bed looks like a dog's nest. He roams once more
through the house looking for food, finds a slightly moldy but very
edible piece of bread. And then a jar of canned pork and a container
with filtered drinking water. He's hungrier than he realized, so it
turns into gorging. Meanwhile, he's starting to feel more comfortable in the farmer's clothes.

While chewing on the old piece of bread, his eye falls on a pile of
old newspapers. Copies of the regional daily the *Uckermärkischer
Kurier.* The most recent is that of Monday, April 4, 1945. On the
front page is a summary of the news from the frontlines, doused
in war propaganda: "In the Thuringia Forest the brave Wehrmacht
succeeded to stop the enemy's advance." Oh gosh, the Allies already
must've crossed the Rhine.

On his way out, he leaves the doors open. He's ready to follow the
path behind the old shed, when he's startled by a loose-running
horse. The brown horse apparently had been hiding behind the
shed. The animal seems as tame as a lamb, so he hurries to the barn
to fetch a bridle and a short rein. But he finds out that his damaged
body has a hard time mounting the horse.

Like a German farmer driven from his property, Meindert that
afternoon rides on horseback toward the southwest. Behind him
the muted droning of the Russians. In the south and southwest a
different kind of roar. The Americans? That's where he needs to go.
Here and there he manages, none too properly, to get his hands on
some food and drink. That evening at eight o'clock he finds a resting place for himself and the horse in an abandoned barn.

A couple of days later he's already joined a cluster of refugees who
some time ago left the southern Berlin suburb of Schönefeld. They
heard that the Russians have already reached the Oder. Others say
that they're already at the River Spree close to Berlin. "The Russians
are here just to murder and to rape."

A good week and a half after he left the farm not far from the

Oder, his flight is beginning to take its toll. First there's the anxiety and hunger, now there's pain and exhaustion on top of that. He becomes heavy hearted; the ringing in his ears, which had already flared up behind the gun platforms on the eastern front, at times drive him crazy, and now his eyes and lungs give him trouble too. Is it caused by the strong burning smell which accompanies him everywhere? He still manages and makes it across a half caved-in wooden bridge on horseback, though he doesn't know what stream he's crossing.

"A small side-river of the Upper Elbe," he finds out from a fellow fleeing companion. "The Allies already have Regensburg in hand." All right, that direction then.

"The burning smell from a few days ago came from Dresden," someone claims. "The English bombed the whole city to smithereens." From a passer-by – one of the hundreds of loners on the run – he learns that the Americans indeed have established control of Regensburg. "And the Russians have crossed the Ohre."

"The End."

The thunder of the cannons is now accompanied with the ric-ka-ricka-ticka of machinegun fire; the war racket escalates from all directions. Seemingly the Wehrmacht is still resisting to the utmost, under the motto of "rather dead than in Russian hands." It can't be long anymore, and Uncle Sam and Ivan will shake hands.

Four, five times he's stopped by Wehrmacht soldiers, and each time he saves himself with a tale. In perfect German: "They burned my farm down, I'm looking for my wife and kids." But one evening at around eight there's trouble. An armed officer stops him and insolently demands his horse. Meindert realizes at once that he's dealing with a deserter. Because a real farmer will never yield his horse without putting up a fight, he first slides off his horse to read the officer the riot act, but before he knows what hit him he goes down from a blow with the butt end of a gun, and not just any kind of blow. As a reflex he must have raised both arms to protect his head, and that gave him a serious injury, maybe a broken shoulder.

Done in, he's sprawled on the ground. There goes the new owner of his last brother-in-arms, the brown horse. His battle for survival is now challenged to the extreme. He must now be careful with the bold acquisition of food, because he has nothing left with which to pose a threat.

"The Americans are only three miles away."

"Yes, they're in the Bohemian Forest, right across the Czech border here!" There's a catch in the voice. "The Wehrmacht there has already surrendered."

He doesn't really care anymore where he stays; the pain in his shoulder is unbearable. His head is spinning from the roaring and the buzzing. Walking becomes a challenge, but he reaches the village he's been stumbling toward for the last hour. At the most ten houses, not a soul in sight, not even a sparrow or a starling. He can no longer muster the energy to go after some food and drink. He finds shelter in a small dilapidated and sagging gazebo behind the largest home of the hamlet. There's a worn, smelly armchair standing on three legs. Because of his damaged left shoulder he tries to sleep sitting up.

A loud noise awakens him; droning and growling it's coming his way. Heavy tanks. It's as if they're going to rumble right over top of him. Below him the earth begins to shake. Overcome with sleep he wants to dive into a manhole, but there is no manhole. With arrow-like stabs of pain he gropes for the door handle of the gazebo, gets the door open, and sees some four monks in brown tunics standing in the garden. With hands folded in front of them they stand reverently under the flowering apple trees. And behind them, high above the hawthorns, a waving flag with stars and stripes moves slowly past.

An hour later he sits with the gray monks at a modest lunch table. He's landed in a small Franciscan monastery. He has no idea what's awaiting him, and it doesn't matter to him either. Whatever will be will be.

After a sour-tasting sandwich and a mug of surrogate coffee from the Franciscan brethren, he stumbles outside and tries to head in the same direction as the colossal caravan of rolling American materiel. No one on the camouflaged tanks, armored vehicles, and trucks seems to pay any attention to the reed-thin and bent-over trudging farmer. He hobbles on in clouds of swirling dust.

To the left of him is the American 90th Infantry Division of the Third American Army under the command of George Patton, the general, who according to the stories, believes in reincarnation and for that reason alone is not afraid of the devil. There's no end to the droning and rumbling, no end to the afternoon. But then he can't go on anymore.

The Meeting

When he comes to and opens his eyes, he sees only the wheel of a car, then a pair of soldier shoes.

"Hey you!" It sounds threatening. He tries to look around, but the spring sun shines right in his face. Words he can't understand confuse him; he tries to get up, but doesn't make it. An officer comes on the scene, at least an important dude, who grabs him vigorously by the sore shoulder. Groaning, he drops down from the pain, but he's ordered to stand and put both hands on the hood of a jeep. The metal is too hot to touch. Right in front of him arises a large white star, behind him he hears the officer who searches him from top to bottom.

"As thin as a rake!" There's laughter.

The officer moves his victim a half turn so that he can look at him from very close up. Then he waves for his driver, who pops from behind the wheel, lifts him up as if he were a toddler of four, and plops him in the jeep in the seat next to his.

Fifteen minutes later he's dropped off in front of a huge factory building with tall, open sliding doors. He tries to have a look but is nearly helpless with pain from his neglected shoulder. The officer and his driver jump back into the jeep and drive on.

A couple of soldiers, seemingly without rank, appear to have been given charge of him. "Take your clothes off!" When did he last change clothes? He's not sure where he should start; he has a hard time getting his shoes off, one of the men has to help.

"And now off with your clothes!" No matter how hard he tries, he can't get his pants off while standing. Someone shoves a chair in his direction; it seems like they're grossed out by him. While seated he manages to get his pants off and tries, when ordered, to get his undershirt with long sleeves off over his neck, but because of the injured shoulder is unable to. Then he gets help and it feels like the

152

whole arm is torn from his body. He howls with pain and falls over on his knees. "My shoulder."

"It's his shoulder."

He loses consciousness momentarily, but he comes around again when they direct him to a separate space in the huge building. One of the men pretends to pull him along by the string of the plover whistle. When he hears laughter, he panics. No, no more torture like that at Hindenburgstrasse 78 in Münster. He tries to raise his left arm in surrender and at the same time show his SS sign in his arm pit, but he's blacking out again from the pain.

He stands naked with his back turned to a high cement wall when they come back with a bucket full of water. They pour some over his body; they avoid the sore shoulder when they rub him with soft soap and wash him. When he's cautiously dried, someone comes with a kind of bike pump to spray him with DDT powder. They can blow him down with it.

"Poor devil, look at that left shoulder, it's blue as hell." The man who says it now grabs him by his long, grown-out flaxy hair and looks him in the eyes. "Nothing left to offer. So we'll take some time to admire your naked acorn." The man points to his sex organ.

His squadron had made sure he knew what this would be all about: checking for sexual diseases like gonorrhea.

"OK! He doesn't even have pubic lice."

"Is he a faggot then?"

"A fucking forced laborer, you mean." He has to guess what they're talking about. Yes, a bit later they're talking about "transfer," he has to be turned over to the authorities. They coax him along to the warehouse of the factory that's been set up like a barracks. Here they fling him clean army underwear, a pair of socks, and pale-green washed pants and shirt. The two men help to get his clothes on, but halfway the pain in his shoulder is no longer bearable, and he passes out.

When he comes to, he's on a bunk bed in a large dormitory and appears to be a part of a bunch of skinny forced laborers whom the Americans have raked together. Apparently to help them recuperate. Most of them are dressed in the same neutral outfit that he's wearing. By the sound of it, some of them are Dutch; one of the men introduces himself as Jan Terhorst from Dordrecht. And there's a Harm, from Winschoten. "Did you work in the Messerschmitt factories too?"

"I believe so, but they've beaten me, I can't remember anything anymore."

American cigarettes are passed around. No stories, they come later, or maybe never. A cigarette is offered to him, silently; when he doesn't react fast enough, one is shoved into his mouth. Suddenly he's nauseated: from the cigarette, from the situation, from himself – it's as if he doesn't want to live anymore. Through his tears he sees light, sunlight, but he doesn't want light anymore.

Later, when he's apparently been temporarily out of it again, he sits on a wooden bench in a walled-in garden. A bright new spring day? A mild summer evening? The plover whistle! Yes, he's still wearing it on his chest. He notices the smell of green soap, it brings him back to his childhood years when his mom let him use the tub.

Just above him a flowering branch of a hawthorn hangs over the old garden wall. Farther on, an American soldier is slumped back in a chair with his eyes closed, enjoying the sun. In the middle of the small lawn a table with a chair beside it. On the table, some stuff, it looks like a big scissors, or a knife with a shiny handle. A wave of fear tears through him.

Now a tall American in a sharply creased khaki uniform appears in the garden. An imposing figure. A couple of stripes on his upper arm, no stars on the collar. Maybe a corporal, but then an impressive one.

"Yes," he shouts. The slumbering soldier pretends to be startled, then takes his seat on the chair next to the small table. The corporal in khaki opens a small container and begins to lather the soldier

154

with the shaving brush, and after that to shave and cut hair. When he's finished, the khaki man looks for the first time in Meindert's direction and says: "Your turn, poor devil!"

At first he doesn't take it seriously, but apparently it's his turn to get a shave and a haircut. When he sits and points to his sore shoulder, the barber nods with understanding and begins to cut. It feels like not much hair will be left on his noggin. Only when he's shaving, talk resumes.

"Where are you from?"

It takes a while before Meindert has his answer ready. "The Netherlands."

"The Netherlands!" The American keeps on shaving and wants to know just where he's from in the Netherlands.

"Friesland."

The man in khaki puts the razor on the table with the foam still on. "Well, then just talk Frisian to me, I speak and understand the language of my folks a little." Meindert hears Frisian the American way. "Dad and Mom came over in 1911 from a town with a stubby tower, and the name of the town is Hichtum."

"My folks are from there too!"

"Your folks and my folks both from Hichtum? Let me tell you that my grandma was very high on that town, because such amazing people lived there. Like the man who wanted to be free as a bird, but even though he could at last sing just as beautiful as a bird, he never became a free bird."

"That was Meindert Boorsma, my grandpa, I'm named after him."

It's a day later. For both men, talking Frisian is the song of the lark which tries to serenade the last turf of its lost land; they exchange stories in the language both of them haven't heard or spoken in a long time. The ghost of a stuffed water curlew flies through the garden, like the comfort bird which after its death lived on for years on the mantelpiece of Nanno's Grandpa Hizkia and Grandma Ytsje. There's the sound of a church hymn running through the walled-in garden, a psalm that a grandma sang to her grandson.

"Yes, do you know what Grandma Ytsje sang when my folks would now and then feel the pangs of their separation from house and home again?" She would sing:

Through the night of grief and worry
Treads the band of pilgrims on.

The stories are continued in the soldiers' large mess hall, then again on the bench in the garden. They talk about that singular Grandpa Meindert, who as a boy with the girl Ytsje conceived of the idea that there was such a thing as a comfort bird. It was needed in a country where the children could be happy with a couple of manure-smeared tufts of sheep's wool.

Johannes and Pytsje's Meindert is willing to try to draw for Douwe and Geartsje's Nanno how the houses in the village surrounded the tower and maybe still do. And then, at last, the plover whistle is hauled out and there in the walled-in garden the sound is heard of the bird's wistful song for the land where it was hatched but that it lost along the way.

"What a deep longing runs through that song," Nanno observes.

Meindert wants to tell of the terrible truth he carries with him, that he has lost his country for good, but he does not dare bring up that confession. Shaking, he sits as the loser next to the victor.

After some ten days Meindert observes Nanno D. Hiemstra consult with an adjutant of the American military police. It looks like they're in agreement: that Meindert should go home, that as road marker guide* he can move in the direction of the Netherlands with

---

* The Germans had strewn the roads with mines; road markers indicated their placement, hence the convoys needed a guide to help them stay within the road markers.

the next troop transport. That forced laborer fellow has a better command of the German language than most of the American staff officers, so that he can be of help with the mega project of directing American army materiel to the Port of Antwerp. That way he can still make himself useful on his home journey. The poor devil may be skinny as a rail, but he's getting to the point of having a bit of color back on his cheeks.

Nanno brings him to the gigantic depot in the jeep, where the numerous columns of men and materiel stand ready for the journey home. And at the last minute there is also a sergeant with the necessary papers and instructions for the road marker guide. For the hundreds of men in the huge barracks who are at the point of the final take-off, excitement rules the order of the day. One after the other platoon springs to attention, and after that the work is done.

Above all the shouting Meindert hears gusts of band music. There comes the band now, marching in a swinging step into the big barracks. The brass band is accompanied by a male choir of hundreds of men waving farewell:

> *So will you please say hello*
> *To the folks that I know*
> *Tell them I won't be long*
> *They'll be happy to know*
> *That as you saw me go*
> *I was singing this song*

As they walk to the jeep together, Nanno says: "Go home and do what the men just now sang and played for us, give my greetings to my people, the people of Friesland, and tell them that I'm fine... They'll be happy to know."

Time to shake hands. Nanno adds: "Meindert, whistle for me one more time the song of the comfort bird."

He tries to, for a moment there's a sound, then it's only tears.

EPILOGUE

It is January 3, 2012; the wind is rising, a storm is on the way. Should there still be a lost wandering soul roaming around, then it's in the town with the stubby tower. I have to climb the tower of Hichtum, want to venture in front of the gaping belfry window. For through that opening there's been enough joy, hope, and sorrow pealed over the land by now.

On the stoop in front of the church door the wind gusts try their best to change my mind. The weather-beaten monument has been changed into a wind machine, the force of the wind tries to deny me entrance, but I fight back and struggle my way in.

Inside the church the wind cries a prayer; I smell the salty incense smoke which from the sea wafts across the wet plains, walk over the vaults of rich, ruling farmers that have been sealed with such massive mausoleum marble that their trust in resurrection must have been firm as a rock.

In the oakwood benches next to the dead the living from the past rise before me. I see the farm wives from the hamlets of Syswert and Himert show off their red corals and casque; in front of the pulpit I stand face to face with John the Evangelist who in the form of a bird of prey speaks to the congregation. The preacher stands on a blue-painted world globe to put his parishioners in their place. Why that lofty language? Who are his parishioners?

I watch the worn-out cow milkers and farm hands who know their place on hard, plain benches. On the other side of the aisle sit their humble women, including in the first row, just now bending forward, Ytsje Namminga-Wytsma. It's as if she's still carrying the yoke with the heavy bread baskets with her. Even when singing psalms she can't keep her eyes off the globe on which the evangelist stands preaching. And then, suddenly, she sees it and knows that the earth is not flat but round. Oh mercy, the earth has yet another side. Here and now Ytsje is shown the path to the New World, to her land of deliverance. In Rotterdam the boat lies ready for departure to America.

It is cold in the thousand-year-old church. Behind the high windows the swaying bald tree crowns signify that the weather has turned rowdy. Above the storm gusts I hear the groaning of the steamship on the ocean. And in the homeland, in the church benches with empty places, Meindert Birdie the plover catcher sits to catch up on sleep. Meindert dreams his own dream; he stayed home because he still had hope that the land of his birth would become the land of his contentment. But his dream wavers and makes him an indecisive man. When he's away he wants to go back home, and when he's home he wants to go away again. That makes him at times so doubt-ridden and irritable that he can't stand John the preacher proclaiming the Word of God in the shape of the cruelest bird of prey – the eagle. Why doesn't this shepherd stand there as a bird of passage in search of the Better Land?

Meindert Birdie is in the mood for rubbing it in with the noble gentlemen of the church: "As long as there's such damn little justice in this world, the proclaimer of God's Word should not stand on such a high pedestal as a bird of prey."

I discover the small round window through which those who had been branded as pagan sinners could still get a glimpse of what was happening in church from their spot in the churchyard. The window meanwhile has been bricked-up, but as I leave the church I see the last outcasts slaving away in all kinds of weather. Close to the cistern they stand. The cistern. With thanks to the church the hundred souls or so of Hichtum will not die of thirst even in the driest summer. The poor, who hardly have a roof above their heads and therefore are also hardly able to catch the heavenly rainwater in a cistern, may fetch a bucketful of water from the church for a nickel.

It irritates Meindert, and he doesn't mind letting the church warden know that: "I would rather drink from the ditch than pay you a cent for God's water."

162

I'm climbing the tower of Hichtum, up the steps that have been worn down by twenty generations of bell-tollers, flag-raisers, and men in hiding during the war. Right before me I see, written with a carpenter's pencil, a sign of past life: a hardly readable farewell greeting from another couple of people who took the boat to America – Nammen H. Namminga, Douwe J. Hiemstra. I see the ticking of the four centuries old clockwork; with all the racket of nature I don't hear it. Imperturbable, the mechanism moves only the hour hand. The deliberations of Hichtum's oldest church warden did not extend to Hartwert, but close to home: count in a timeframe of centuries not the seconds or minutes, for when it is our time, then it is our time. Two steps higher the din of the storm comes roaring through the tower's belfry openings. I venture in front of one of the gaping holes and what I observe in a glimmer is a flight of geese that waffles between flying on or staying. The soaked field takes on the ruddy shape of a golden plover. Here and there a tuft of bare thicket, but it's all exactly where it belongs.

I'm almost blown away from the belfry window, hold myself upright by the cold bronze of one of the two clocks. The big one shows a crack and is out of tune, the way churches can rupture and fall out of tune. Next to it sways the little clock with which women and children were mourned.

On the other side of the tower Kleaster Canal comes into my view, the water that runs like a silver strip to the Pig's Skin, the farmhouse where my great-great grandfather Lieuwe Sjoerds Mensonides struggled through the agricultural depression of the 1880s with his almost thirty years younger Ybeltsje Faber. Frugal Lieuwe, who could light all three of his cattle barn lamps with one match. A mile farther on, at the end of a glistening white plain, the farm on the Hunia Road where my grandfather Hylke Bonnes Hylkema farmed successfully with grandmother Wietske Hofstee. Until Hylke with unshared grief for whatever reason gave himself back to the earth.

Forty-five degrees further to starboard the hamlet of Laad en Saad where to my surprise I see the farm where my great grandfather Bouwe Hantsjes Speerstra and great grandmother Richtsje Harmens Boersma were married and fifty years later celebrated their wedding anniversary with a great flock of descendants. Laad en Saad, that is to say: go and multiply. Hardly half a mile to the west the farm of my grandpa Bartele Bouwes Speerstra and grandma Jeltsje Sjoerds Oppedijk. The farm later became the property of my good dad and mom, Bouwe Barteles Speerstra and Aaltsje Hylkes Hylkema. There, in the hamlet of Iemswâlde, they frugally survived the terrible 30s and later in its shadow fulfilled their stewardship.

All of them, they stayed through the years where they were and what they were: farmer and farmer's wife in the land where the dike embraced not only the land but also themselves. Their dreams reached to the sea dike, not beyond. They sang of it as their fatherland, at weddings, coffees, and funerals: "Where the dike the land embraces."

But on those farms the hardworking farm workers and cow milkers also had dreams and hopes; they felt themselves embraced by more than just a dike. Their roofs were too small to catch a just portion of heaven's water; they took the chance of crossing the sea dike. There, between the homeland and the land of dreams, the cruel path. "Sea, sea, you wide sea, who knows what misfortunes and woe are hidden in thee."

NANNO HIEMSTRA

In South Dakota and later in Wisconsin Nanno Hiemstra would hardly talk about the war until his 70th year. He did often regale the family surrounding him with stories about the old Friesland that his parents had told him about. But for years he kept silent about the horrors of war, till one of his grandchildren kept asking him about it. Then it came out that he had already entrusted some stories to paper.

In March 1942, after the Japanese had destroyed the American Navy fleet in Pearl Harbor some three months before, Nanno was drafted into the service. His twin brother Lawrence had just become an independent farmer and was exempted. "I went and I, oh miracle, came back."

He survived the Normandy invasion, the Ardennes offensive, and the battles in Germany to the other side of the Czechoslovak border. "That I was spared again and again for 332 days of battle is inconceivable. However grateful I am for that, till my death I will also lug the horrors with me."

His 90th Infantry Division lost 6,500 men, suffered 15,000 wounded, and hundreds missing in action.

After Germany surrendered on May 8, 1945, he had to stay in Europe till September of that year to help dismantle the sizeable American armed forces and to help in the logistics of the transport of materiel. Due to having his hearing damaged from the shellfire, he was supposed to have a hearing test before embarking in Antwerp. There was a good chance that he would be granted a modest but permanent war injury benefit. "But I saw the ship in the harbor that could sail me home. And waiting for me in Wisconsin were my young wife Alice, and the little girl I knew only from a picture, who was born when a year-and-a-half earlier I crossed the Atlantic Ocean on the way to war."

And that's how nothing came of the intended visit to Hichtum, which he and his brothers and sisters had heard such amazing stories about.

"It was already Indian Summer in Wisconsin; on the train platform of Sharon stood my beloved with little Lorraine. The little one was at first scared of the tall stranger and started to cry, and I cried with her, because it was as if I was being born anew, began to live anew. And there were my parents too; there stood my past and my future."

Within three days of his homecoming, Nanno was back to work.

As Grandma Ytsje would have said: "The work has to pull you through."

Nanno was blessed to have a winsome partner in Alice (Aaltsje) Coehoorn, an Iowa-born farmer's daughter. The household expanded with eight more healthy children who for the most part would also become farmer and farmer's wife.

Nanno's mother Geartsje Namminga passed away on May 27, 1954. She almost reached the age of 75. Father Douwe Hiemstra died two years later at the age of 77. Grandma Ytsje had already been laid to rest in the Depression year of 1934, when in South Dakota the Dust Bowl had cast a pall on everyone.

In 1981 Nanno and Alice decided to take a trip to France, Germany, and, – at the end – to the Netherlands. He couldn't avoid it, soldier Hiemstra stood again on Utah Beach, speechless and overtaken by his own emotions. When the memories of war hit close, Hiemstra's personality proved him to be a man of few words.

The American military cemeteries were not forgotten. The trip continued, through the Ardennes, across the Mosel to the Rhine, until they also landed in the town of Bodenwöhr by the Czech border where in the post-war liberation he had had a curious meeting. The final leg of their trip ended in Friesland. In the first place, of course, to see the village with the stubby tower and the old terp full of names and stories which from Hichtum would live on far beyond the Hudson. But also to reconnect with that emaciated young Frisian who had suddenly shown up one day in the barber chair. To their great disappointment, no one was able to help them locate Meindert Boorsma. They could only wonder what had happened to him.

Nanno Hiemstra's high military honors included the Bronze Star, the Invasion Arrowhead, and all five Battle Stars: for Normandy, Northern France, the Ardennes, Rhineland, and Central Europe. The French War Cross he received from the hands of General Charles de Gaulle.

Each year, from his 75th to his 92nd, WWII veteran Hiemstra visited schools in Wisconsin to tell students "about the preciousness of freedom and about the high price that sometimes has to be paid for that freedom."

In the spring of 2012 Nanno Hiemstra, 93 in the meanwhile, and his wife Alice (91) celebrated with all nine children and more than eighty grand- and great-grandchildren their 70th wedding anniversary. They celebrated first in Texas, where each year they had escaped the Midwest cold for three months in wintertime; and they did it again in Ripon, WI, where they had made their home for all these years. In their retirement years they enjoyed living independently and in good health on their son's farm. It was the man himself who in the summer of 2012 still drove the two of them to their Reformed Church in a village close by. And when near lunchtime he'd drive back into their own yard, he'd routinely lapse back in the old language of long ago: "Grandma Ytsje would say: 'Wy binne wer thús' - 'We're home again.'"

Nanno Hiemstra died on May 20, 2015. He was 95 years old. His wife Alice died on March 9, 2017, she was almost 95. Alice, still in good health at the time, traveled to the Netherlands in April 2016 with eleven family members. The people of Hichtum surprised the visitors with a ceremony in the 800-year old village church, for 'our liberator Hiemstra'.

MEINDERT BOORSMA

In the early summer of 1945 Meindert Boorsma began his own return from Germany. First as a 'road marker guide,' later as a kind of stowaway among the Americans who after the war began their homeward journey by the thousands through a damaged Germany. "I had had a feeling for a long time already that I was heading toward a lot of trouble. I really had only one wish left: one hour of peace in Friesland, one hour with Dad and Mom in the houseboat on the Workum Tow Canal below Nijhuzum."

He literally could not be himself when he had arrived in Belgium among the liberators of Europe. With his ugly secret he fled from the column long before reaching Antwerp and landed in the south of the Netherlands. By then he had been on the run for more than three months already. After some four days he picked up a ride to Leeuwarden. "I got the feeling that I could bump into trouble at any moment. 'Where did you come from, what were you up to during the war, where did you celebrate liberation?'

And then in my mind I had the answer ready: 'I served in a foreign military, what do you say about that!' I felt it coming: that would not be taken too lightly."

From Leeuwarden he was able to ride with the carrier from Blesse to the Sneek corner below Reduzum. It was a mild summer evening in June when he started walking to Sneek.

"I smelled the scent of cut grass, of pungent hay, and was nearly dizzy from it. The sun was setting so beautifully, the same sun which had risen so beautifully when I was milking by Harm and Sietske in the meadow, that moment when the war started. The evening dew stole through the field gullies, around me I saw white-edged fields, and I thought: this is heaven, but then a heaven which will not take me in."

How long had his escape from Northwest Russia taken? Dead tired and hungry he arrived in the night in Skearnegoutum. One house still had light showing. He saw a white shape in the dim glow of a kerosene lamp, a man in white underwear. Meindert took a chance and knocked on the window. The door opened at once, the way it does when a new freedom has been ushered in.

"Meindert! You here!" He's standing right in front of Red Simen, a former farm worker in the area. He had once spent a fall season spreading manure with Red Simen.

"Everybody thinks that you were killed on the eastern front," Simen stammers, while sleep-drunk he puts a foot in the leg of his pants. "Dear boy, you should try to get to that poor old soul of yours as soon as possible, your mother in the houseboat isn't expecting it anymore. Because your dad isn't there anymore either, you sure must've found out that the old Kaiser came to a bad end. And do you know that well before liberation they burned down Rintsje Haagsma's beautiful farm? No wonder that he made an end to it a few days ago in the Workum weigh house*. You know something? I'm going to rustle up a bike for you, then you can ride in a good hour to your dear mom in the houseboat. Come on, boy, make yourself comfortable in the hay in the meanwhile."

Red Simen did not come back with a bike but with three men from what had been the anti-Nazi Dutch Interior Forces. An hour later he was confined in an old tobacco factory in Sneek that had been converted to a house of detention.

They wouldn't spare him here; every night he heard that someone was roughly dragged from his cell, and every time the commotion ended with a gunshot. And again and again he was told the next day that someone was placed against the wall and that it would be his turn soon.

When it got that far, he asked if he would be allowed a short visit with his mom in the houseboat. His request was denied. Meindert's last hour seemed to have arrived; he walked himself to the wall.

"Someone who had partially covered his face with a red handkerchief pointed his carbine at me, but at the last second he shot in the air. I will tell you honestly: I experienced it as a disappointment."

Before they were going to be transported to a penal camp in Sondel as political delinquents, they were told in no uncertain terms how the Germans had treated their resistance fighters. "Before I was transported, a policeman came to me. Policeman Blijham. 'Tomorrow I'll bring you to your mom in the houseboat. What they will do with you after that, I have nothing to do with.' I didn't be-

---

* The Workum weigh house was in use as a police station with holding cells.

lieve anybody, but Blijham kept his word."

Meindert at the Nijhuzum Bridge came to the 'Meadow and Water,' and indeed there was no dad anymore. A mother, yes. Pytsje Boorsma-Jongsma at first couldn't utter a word, didn't know better than that her son had been killed in the winter of 1944 near Leningrad. And here he stood before her. A man of 6'3" who weighed only 115 pounds.

The reputation of Johannes had grown worse during the war. Supposedly he had stood guard as a national socialist Nazi sympathizer in front of the Workum distribution office, where men in the resistance hoped to get their hands on ration stamps for people in hiding.

Right after Workum was liberated on April 17, 1945, Johannes had been arrested. While awaiting trial, he with others who had been on the wrong side had to dig up live grenades along the railroad track between Workum and IJlst and take them away with horse and wagon. It went without a glitch till Thursday morning, May 17. A grenade exploded which had been placed on the wagon by Johannes himself. He was killed instantly.

Right before that accident, one of the guards had assured him that he should figure on "twelve years cell."

Widow Pytsje Boorsma-Jongsma was informed a day and a half after the accident, on Friday night, May 18 near bedtime, that the burial of her husband needed to take place that same week. Thus the next day – on Saturday afternoon, May 19 – in Hichtum during milking time, Johannes Boorsma was laid to rest in the place not far from the bricked-up window and the cistern, where his dad Meindert had lain buried with his plover whistle since 1912. The parent's grave now was cleared to make room for the son.

Besides son Meindert, his daughters, who were then working as farm maids, were not able to attend because of the time of day.

Meindert got four years' penal camp detention, spending time in Sondel, Veenhuizen, and Westerbork. There he became known as a hard worker. In the course of 1948 he was granted a provisional release for good behavior. In the late summer of 1990 his Dutch citizenship was restored through the advocacy of a couple of Heidenskip farmers.

On Thursday April 13, 1950 he married Jacoba Muizelaar from Koudum. After they had a stillborn child, they were blessed with four healthy children who all turned out well: Johannes, Jacob, Albert, and Tytsje.

"Though for me it was never 'after the war,' I can say that I nevertheless experienced a lot of love and friendship."

Meindert was at first a steady farm worker, later on he went into more temporary work because he couldn't do without catching plovers. He did that with the implements that had been those of his dad and grandpa.

When his wife died on May 21, 1993, Meindert was a broken man. A good year later, on September 3, 1994, he passed away in the Teatske Seniors Home in Blauhûs. I had visited him there just two weeks earlier. With great animation he told me then how on November 5, 1964 in the Flait below Molkwar he had caught a flight of 44 plovers. "And the best thing was, there was a beautiful curlew among them."

ACKNOWLEDGMENTS

Without the cooperation and openness of the American farmer and war veteran Nanno Hiemstra (South Dakota, 1919) and Meindert Boorsma, farmhand and bird catcher, born in the same year near Ysbrechtum, I would not have been able to write this story. I am deeply grateful for their cooperation.

I met Mr. Hiemstra for the first time in 2010 in Ripon, Wisconsin. Once he started talking, he proved to be a calm but gifted narrator with an impressive memory; a man of character and now 93, who also after our conversations would assist me in word and deed.
I spoke at different times with Meindert Boorsma well before his death in 1994. We had become friends. In 1948 – I was then an adolescent – I understood that Meindert had been on the wrong side during the war. I wondered then already why none in my area seemed to be curious about his past and his ups and downs. With me – a curious neighbor boy – it was different. Through the years I would find out how he was dragged into a war and what kind of terrible consequences that had. The same way I would find out that on the other side of the ocean another young man was dragged into the war – but this time not on the wrong side.
Later, after I became acquainted with our liberator Nanno Hiemstra, I discovered that the grandparents of Nanno and Meindert had been neighbors in Hichtum and that their history shared so many parallels. For the storyteller the time was ripe to write the history which began under circumstances of poverty.
Two laborer households, two fellow sufferers in declining times, dreaming of a better world. Each chooses – insofar as there is anything to choose – his own way. The time would teach them that for the wanderer in search of a better future, there is no clear path, but that as one wanders the path gradually emerges. The paths of life

run far apart, but through bizarre coincidences would cross again.

Before and during the writing of this book I received from the Hiemstras and Boorsmas a number of family documents on loan. Debbie N. Hiemstra from Oshkosh, WI, successfully went in search of old letters and memoranda. Regarding the Hiemstras, the following documents constituted an important signpost:

- *The Memories and Life Stories of the Children and Grandchildren Hiemstra/Namminga. 1979, Springfield, SD.*
- *The Nanno & Alice Hiemstra Story. Ripon, WI.*
- *The Story and Family Tree of Hezekiah D. Hiemstra. Springfield, SD.*
- *The Stories of a World War II Veteran. By Hazel Blocker, 1992.*

A number of accounts in this book are based on orally delivered family stories. In South Dakota singular anecdotes about the people in the town with the stubby tower still make the rounds. Now and then an aphorism from Grandma Ytsje Namminga-Wytsma sneaks in too. I realize that through time, language, and fantasy a distorted image can develop, but here and there I couldn't avoid making use of it.

To describe the weal and woe of the Boorsma family, I was greatly aided by the candid and consistently kept diary of Johannes Boorsma. This 'Tagebuch', which gives a good insight in the life and work of the Frisian milkers in the German dairies, covers the first three decades of the 20th century.

Hereby I want to express my sincere thanks to Johannes's grandson Albert Meindert Boorsma for his help. During my writing I kept receiving relevant information from him from the valuable family archive.

In my search for stories, sources, and backgrounds in Hichtum and surroundings I received significant support from town historian Lolle R. Baarda from Burchwert and the late Dieuwke N. Boorsma from Bolsward. For a number of accounts in the first three chapters I was able to make use of old documents from our own family. Those of my great grandmother Klaske Mensonides were especially helpful. With help from archivist Otto Gielstra from Makkum I was able to clarify various things from the archive of the former municipality of Wûnseradiel.

For a fragment in the prologue about the time when men went into hiding and the murder of Justin Gerstner (alias Douwe Elzinga) in our hamlet of Iemswâlde, I could depend, besides on my own observation (I was then a boy of eight), on what Bouke and Sjoerd Buwalda had told me earlier. They witnessed the drama; it would haunt them till their death. Their information is consistent with what I heard in 1994 from Lucas Dreese from Amstelveen who was in hiding at the time. I also want to thank the Gerstner family from the Göteborg in Sweden for their information about 'Douwe.'

I had the privilege in the fall of 1995 of being present with the parties mentioned above in the synagogue of Amstelveen for a memorial service, dedicated to Justin Gerstner.

It almost goes without saying that I also made much use of the archives of the Leeuwarder Courant and the earlier Nieuwsblad van Friesland – commonly known by its readers as the Hepkema. Added to all that is, of course, the treasure house of Tresoar.

In conclusion I want to make special mention of Jaap and Janke Hiemstra from Heerenveen. They were the ones who in the spring of 2010 pointed me to the existence of Jaap's full cousin and war veteran Nanno. Yet that same week I flew to America to 'fetch a story.'

In 2011 the first printing of The Comfort Bird appeared, but then in shorter form. It was issued in limited circulation as a gift for the Frisian Book Month.

In conclusion I want to thank the following persons and agencies: S.G. Alberda, Sneek; Jozef Aszmann, Wiebelsheim (Germany); Jan Bouwhuis, Bolsward; Tine Bouwsma-Kaspersma †, Workum;

Ron Brands (Archive Passenger lists Holland-America/Rotterdam Municipality Archive); Simon A. Duursma and Karel P. Eringa †, Burchwert; Bouwe Jansen, Koudum; Bertus Jellema, Workum; Bert van de Kam, Griendtsveen; Uwe Klare, Sterkrade (Germany); Cor Kooistra, Nijlân; Friedje Kroeze-Boorsma, Hindeloopen; Oscar Lübke, Frankfurt (Oder) (Germany); Jurjen van der Meer, Terkaple; Peter van der Meer, Bolsward; Namminga family, Winsum-Leeuwarden; Noordenbos family, It Heidenskip; Theunis Piersma, Gaast; Dieter Schlüter †, Berlin; Wim Schrijver, Hallum; Koos Schulte, Sneek; Freark Smink, Britswert; Gerrit Twijnstra, It Heidenskip; Lolke Jacobs Wytsma, Mullum; and the IJ. Ykema family, Hichtum.

Selected Bibliography

Brinks, Herbert J. – *Write Back Soon. Letters from Immigrants in America.* Grand Rapids, 1986.

Galema, Annemieke – *Frisians to America, 1880-1914. With the Baggage of the Fatherland.* Groningen, 1996.

Lucas, Henry S. – *Dutch Immigrant Memoirs and Related Writings.* Assen, 1955.

Speerstra, Hylke – *Cruel Paradise. Life Stories of Dutch Emigrants.* Grand Rapids, 2005.

Van Hinte, Jacob – *Netherlanders in America. A study of Emigration and Settlement in the Nineteenth and Twentieth Centuries in the United States of America.* Groningen, 1926.

CPSIA information can be obtained
at www.ICGtesting.com
Printed in the USA
BVOW11s1940060417
480346BV00002B/2/P